# NAKEDER THAN THOU

David Leddick

Second Edition

White Lake Press
*Miami Beach*

**Table of Contents**

**"No One Is Whom They Seem"**
**—Catherine, Comtesse**
**Contant De Cazas**

## Introduction

I must explain that this book has been compiled by me from material collected by my neighbor in the French country town of Terrassée, D. D. Abercrombie. Miss Abercrombie wasn't the kind of person you would have called "Ms." She was named Dorothy Danforth Abercrombie by her parents. She was a tall and slender person (would you have called her "thin"?) of a type you would not have easily classified as American. She was from Canton, Ohio, originally, she once told me. But the citizens of Terrassée, when they saw her gliding by, always referred to her as "La Grande Anglaise." She did have something of the outspoken nature of an English eccentric.

She had been an editor at *Vogue* magazine when she first came to Terrassée. Perhaps she came on a fashion photo shooting. She bought a very old house there facing the abbey of Terrassée and evidently did much of the renovation herself. I came there some ten years later and bought a house around the corner from her. I don't know if you could say we were friends, but because I am a writer she talked to me in some detail when she was trying to disentangle a mystery involving someone who had lived previously in the house she had bought. She had no great skill at writing herself, but she spoke to me at great length during the several years she spent collecting material, taking notes, and recording in notebooks what she found.

I have taken this material, which she left with me, and simply put it in the order of her own explorations. Much of her writing she left in the form of notes put in diary form. Some of the material she told to me I have attempted to put in similar diary form.

The mystery which unfolds in this book is further deepened by D. D. Abercrombie's own disappearance. I have no reason to think she is dead. Friends have told me that she has moved to Montevideo in Uruguay. There is some feeling that she followed a man there. This I do not know, but I should add that there was nothing virginal about D. D. Abercrombie, though she was a single woman and I believe was never married. I would have thought she was capable of quite a lot of sexual refinement. D. D., if you ever read this book, please contact me. I'm keeping the royalties for you.


—David Leddick

**Chapter 1**
**Bring Out Your Dead**


From D. D. Abercrombie's Journal:
"We found a skeleton in the cave," the boys said.
"Forget that stuff and come to lunch. This isn't an Agatha Christie novel," I said.
"No, no, we really did. There's a small skull and everything!" my nephew Nathan exclaimed. He was excited. He loves treasure hunts. Behind him his older brother Alexander loomed. He was excited too.
"I want you to go right back down in the cave and cover it up and come to the table." I knew exactly the effect of the news that I had a skeleton in my cave would have on the village of Terrassée-sur-Loir, where I lived part of every year. I was brought up in a very similar town in Ohio. One thousand inhabitants of whom you only ever saw thirty. The rest were lurking behind their nylon lace curtains watching their neighbors, longing for a little excitement. The news would quickly be garbled into the story that a body had been found in my basement, or cave, as it is called in France. Surely they would think it was recently interred, and I was most certainly responsible for it. My nephews were living a Robert Louis Stevenson novel. I would have to live the reality. I was only too aware of what bored little small-town minds can construct.
I like living in Terrassée. I've been here quite a while. Although I am an American, I'm known as "La Grande Anglaise" (The Tall English Woman) and am now quite accepted, although I have never been invited to dinner in anyone's home. After seventeen years here, the boulangère has begun to call me by name. My last name, of course. I can't imagine what it would take for a villager to use my first name.
So as far as a body in the basement is concerned, the news can't leak out. It just has to be forgotten. I had almost forgotten it myself by the time my two lanky teenagers had re-emerged, dusty and sulky.
"Please wash your hands," I said. I could tell they were terribly disappointed at my reaction to their news. But there was nothing for it.
My friends, the Panaguas, arrived at this point, clanging the bell above the front door. They entered with wine in a basket. Four bottles. I hoped they were planning to drink most of it at lunch. I let the boys have a glass of wine at dinner but not at lunch. I have very little myself at lunch. The Loire Valley is soporific enough. I don't want to drowse my time away altogether while I'm here. But as it turned out, the body in the cave just below my sitting room wasn't to be ignored as easily as I thought.
Only two days later I took the boys with me to have lunch with the Comtesse Nathalie Bavour de Cazas. She had been born a Comtesse and married Monsieur Bavour. She added her title to his name, although he continued to be plain M. Bavour. Nathalie is older than I am. She certainly looks older and, like most French aristocrats, is very much at ease with Americans and rather likes them. For some reason, we have a kind of chic in their eyes the English don't have. The boys are forced to speak French with her, although she has a smattering of English. They hate having to speak French but, since that's one of the reasons they are with me, it must be suffered through.

La Comtesse doesn't live in the family chateau, Le Rivage, but next door in a very nicely redone farm. Her oldest brother inherited Le Rivage, but did not have the money to maintain it well. Now one of Nathalie's nephews weekends in the lower part of one wing.

At lunch, the Comtesse told us about being brought up by her grandparents at Le Rivage. Her mother had died giving birth to Nathalie and her grandmother took over immediately, raising the baby and her three older brothers in the vast, racketing windiness of the chateau.

Her memories of the Occupation held the boys glued to their seats. When you really want to know something in a foreign language your brain kicks in, and it's amazing how quickly you learn. That's why I always recommend reading pornography when you are learning a new language.

The boys listened intently as she told them about the Germans coming to Terrassée and immediately requisitioning Le Rivage for the officers' billet as it was the largest chateau in the area. The family was given a few hours to pack up and decamp. Fortunately, they had another smaller and even older chateau only a few miles away that they only used for the hunting season. Here they spent the war in a fairly primitive way. There was, of course, no heat except for fireplaces, and France had exceptionally cold winters during the war years. They must have lived very much as their family had two hundred years earlier. Few baths, food cooked over open fires, perhaps there was an old iron range there, no new clothes, scrounging the countryside for food. As she talked I wondered where the Comtesse had gone to school. Her brothers and she probably went to the public school in the village. That might have been the hardest part for them. They don't seem to know anyone in the village, or at least their names never come up. Perhaps they didn't go to school at all.

One day in the summer they heard the Germans had left and went back to Le Rivage. All the dishes and glasses had been broken. They found shards of glass all over the dining room where drinking glasses had been thrown against the wall. Nathalie was particularly distressed by the Germans having taken all the bed linens out into the orchards and ridden their horses over them. There were undoubtedly many, many sheets and pillowcases that had filled the armoires of Le Rivage, as traditionally the laundry was only done at great intervals, and then in enormous amounts. I found this fascinating. I would have loved to see the German officers riding under the trees, ducking their heads to avoid low-hanging branches, trampling the snowy sheets and pillowcases under their horses' hooves. How wondrously strange. Had it really happened? Had they realized that the war was lost and they had to take their anger out on something that was in no way responsible? Like the laundry? The past is curious, isn't it? Inexplicable, and perhaps just as inexplicable to the Ger-man officers stampeding across the white and green of the linen-strewn grass of the orchard.

"Voulez-vous voir Le Rivage?" the Comtesse asked us as we were eat-ing peaches and grapes from the large bowl in the middle of the round dining table. Did we want to see the cha teau? My nephews, the treasure hunters, love any old kind of place, of course. They wanted to go immediately and were already halfway out of their chairs. Nathalie told us as we were going out to our car that her nephew happened to be in residence at the moment in his renovated part of the cha teau, and that she rarely went there. But having talked about it at lunch had put her in the mood to see it with us.

In the car she renewed her lipstick. She has white hair and an upright figure and wears a very brilliant scarlet lipstick. This is not common among the women of the country aristocracy, but the Comtesse lived in Paris when she was married and this is perhaps to remind the others that she has a past of citified chic and sophistication they do not share.

Le Rivage has the look of a late eighteenth-century chateau. The Louis the Sixteenth and Marie Antoinette period. Squarish and somewhat neoclassic. There is a pillared portico over the entrance with an empty niche on either side. The niches are large enough for life-size statues. As we passed them Nathalie said, "The statues are now on the grand staircase of the Chateau de Blois in the Gaston of Orléans wing. He was Louis the Thirteenth's brother. He and his mother, Marie de Medici, were always plotting against poor Louis so he exiled both of them there. Gaston was the father of the Grande Mademoiselle, you know. I always thought she was a lesbian, but evidently not. Her uncle, the king, was homosexual, of course. I've never believed that he was Louis the Fourteenth's father. There was a lot of homosexuality in the Bourbons. Probably that Medici blood." The Comtesse spoke of the royal family as though they had been neighbors and she had known them well.

Now we were in the main entrance hall of the chateau, a large square room with a sweeping staircase at the back. "My grandmother used this as the salon," the Comtesse said. "She had large tapestries she hung in the winter to cut out the drafts, but it was still terribly cold. We huddled around the fireplace." There was a very large fireplace on the right wall. "Originally, this was an open passageway so the carriages could go right through to the courtyard. It was my grandfather who closed it in and put the staircase in place." It all looked much older than something just over a hundred years old.

At this point, the Comtesse's nephew appeared. He was a large, bluff person who had rather smartly done up the ground floor to the left of the entry hall. The Comtesse was pleasant to her nephew but no more so than if he had been a neighbor or not too close a friend. Perhaps she felt that this was still her home and he was something of an intruder. As she showed us the two large rooms that made up his apartment she said, "These were my grandparents' bedrooms." It passed through my mind that it was unusual for bedrooms to be on the ground floor and also unusual for a married couple to sleep separately at that time, but I said nothing. As we entered what had been a bedroom and was now her nephew's sitting room I asked her, "Was this room ever a library?"

The Comtesse turned and looked me squarely in the face. "What an unusual question," she said. "Actually, it was, I believe. In the time of the old Comtesse. She was, let me see, my great-great-grandmother."

"Do you know if it was red?" I asked.

"I believe it was green. Are you experiencing déjà vu?" she said. "Are you one of those people who can conjure up the past? Are you one of those people who believe they have lived previous lives?" She obviously was checking me out to see if I had distressing lower-middle-class tendencies. Perhaps a person who read horoscopes. They would be very un-French and rather inelegant in her view, that was clear.

"Oh, not at all," I said. "I never see or hear ghosts when other people do. I'm very unimaginative, I'm afraid."

"I would not have thought that," the Comtesse said. I did not tell her about Matt's dream.

# Chapter 2
## Matt's Dream

What can I tell you about Matt? Not much. A young man of broad shoulders and narrow waist who had been engaged to renovate my country house. A young American man who had become infatuated with France. He had been a guest in the house as a friend of a friend, and hearing that it needed a lot of interior repainting and plastering, offered to do it for room and board.

I had my reservations and told him that being alone in a four hundred-year-old house in the French winter might not be what he anticipated, and that I would not hold him to his word should he want to depart at any time. He was only twenty-four. He assured me he really wanted to stay.

Matt thrived on renovating the old house. He busied himself peeling off old wallpaper, plastering cracks, repainting walls. I gave him Le Grand Meaulnes to read, and when I was in the country we would drive off to visit some of the sites of Alain-Fournier's book.

One weekend when I arrived he told me he had had a strange dream. In this dream he had been in uniform, a red and white uniform, and had been with a dark-haired woman in a blue dress telling her that he had to leave and go to the war in Spain. The woman was crying. The woman was older than he was and somehow he knew that they had been lovers. "All I really remember about her was that her hair was parted in the middle," he said.

He added, "And somehow I knew it was 1840. And that I was at Le Rivage. We seemed to be in a library. There were lots of books around."

I asked him, "What color were the walls?"

He said, "Red. The room seemed to be red."

"But there was no war with Spain in 1840," I said. Matt shrugged. I went to my room. I had a book there on the kings of France, with an abbreviated history of each of their reigns. There, very much to my surprise, I found there had been a brief war with Spain in 1840 in the reign of Louis-Philippe. The Citizen King. There were no details, but there had been a war.

"Where was the original staircase?" I asked the Comtesse as we moved back through the entry hall.

"In the room that was the library when I was young," the Comtesse said. "Here, through the dining room. My grandmother used the old library as her bedroom." The dining room was being rather elaborately refurbished when we stepped into it. A young woman was painting elaborate flower and wheat designs on the wood-paneled walls. I knew her. She lived directly across the street from me in the village, where she had pined, year after year, for some married man who had never divorced and married her. We nodded and smiled at each other. I wondered if she knew as much about my private life as I knew about hers. Probably.

In the blue-painted library one could still see clearly on the wall where the old staircase had mounted, in the front left-hand corner of the building. It must have been serviceable but clearly was not grand. The high point of Le Rivage's day must have been in the time of the Comtesse's grandfather.

"Where was your father while you were being brought up by your grandparents?" I asked the Comtesse as we left the library for the vast kitchen that stretched out into a left wing behind the main façade.

The Comtesse said, "He was in Paris, of course." Obviously, the Comtesse felt her family history was far better known than it was. I pursued the question no further but wondered, did her father have a mistress in Paris whom he preferred to be with? Did he have an important government position that required his presence there? And if so, why weren't his children with him? Or was there a scandal? About money? About sex? Probably there was no scandal about sex as the French never see anything scandalous about human fragility as it pertains to passion. As it pertains to money, certainly. I was never to have the answers to any of these questions. No one whom the Comtesse and I knew mutually had any more idea than I did. Nor did they have interest. Only I seemed interested in the history of her family. More likely, mutual French friends knew plenty but were not about to discuss it. Particularly with an American. The past is left to bury itself in France.

On the second floor of Le Rivage were the large reception rooms. The main salon was a vast room spreading over the main entrance, and it was in a rather remarkable state of decay. It was difficult to imagine that while the young blonde woman was downstairs painting fresh flowers and stalks of wheat on the wood panels of the dining room, above her was a room in which the ceiling plaster was falling and allowed to lie uncollected on the faded and fraying carpets. The upholstery of the mildly Louis the Fifteenth furniture was equally frayed and faded and a heavy layer of dust lay over everything. The small boxes and framed photographs on the small tables scattered about the room lay under coats of dust too. It was as though someone had walked out before World War I and never returned to move a vase or straighten a picture. The Comtesse did not seem to notice the abandoned quality of the room. I immediately thought of Dickens's Miss Havisham. This would be as she had lived, drifting through in her tattered bridal white.

The Comtesse indicated the paintings on the walls. "My grandmother. My great-grandfather." Low on one wall beside the fireplace she indicated, "My grandfather." Her grandfather had been a very handsome man. In the drawing he had a curly moustache and fair hair and large dark eyes. It was the kind of face that accepted the admiration that was always given it.

"Your grandfather was very handsome," I said. "Everyone always said that," the Comtesse replied in a tone of voice that suggested she was not altogether convinced.

"Are there no portraits of your father here?" I asked her.

"Oh no," she said emphatically.

My nephews exchanged glances. They knew I was sleuthing. They know me well. Their mother, who is very much like me in other ways, does not have my inquisitive qualities and is in no way as interested in other people and their lives as I am. There must have been some scandal associated with the father's departure from his children's lives.

The hall that connected the upper rooms was also littered with bits of falling plaster and covered in dust. The nephew who lived at Le Rivage never sent his cleaning women to this part of the château, that was quite clear. Nor did the Comtesse seem to think this was unfortunate. At the end of the hall she opened a door to show us a bedroom.

"My brothers and I had our rooms in this wing, here, beside the old Comtesse's bedroom." This room was done with walls, bed hangings, and bedcover all in a dark red and white Toile de Jouy fabric. That beautiful cloth that is covered with scenes of small houses, little copses of trees, milkmaids, and farmers in their fields. The bedcover was not in the same design as the walls and the bed hangings, suggesting that it had been replaced at some point. The outer shutters were tightly shut and the light in the room was dim, which probably accounted for the brightness of the color in the cloth. Daylight had not been allowed to fall upon it very much.

"Her bedroom was used as a guest room occasionally in my youth. Not very often," the Comtesse said as she closed the door. She did not show us the rooms once occupied by her brothers and herself.

Downstairs in the back courtyard one could see clearly the bulging back wall of the sweeping staircase in the entry hall, and it was easy to imagine how it must have been when there was a passageway under the upper floor.

"You see, the entire front of the chateau was added to the earlier buildings by my great-great-grandfather at the time he married the first Comtesse. Before then, there was this building that is now the right wing. And the left wing, where the kitchen is, was the housing for the servants and the farmworkers. Le Rivage is just a big farm actually." The Comtesse said this as though she didn't believe it for a minute.

"Where was the first Comtesse from?" I asked her great-great-granddaughter.

"From the south. From near Aix, I believe."

"How did she meet your great-great-grandfather?" I asked.

"Oh, I'm sure that it was arranged. It always was in those days," she answered.

This must have been the woman in blue, I thought. The woman with her hair parted in the middle who wept at her lover's words, knowing he was leaving her as much as he was going to war.

## Chapter 4
## More About Matt

I wrote Matt. This was not such an unusual thing for me to do. I had been very much in love with Matt. Much more than I should have been. There was an enormous difference in our ages. There was absolutely no kind of future in any kind of relationship. It didn't make any kind of sense at all. But, voilà. There you have it. Of course, it turned out badly. Of course, I behaved like a fool. Of course, I got over it. I'm not one of those "Let's be friends" kind of people. More "Let's be enemies." I finally wrote him and said that I was going to have to cut off all contact with him if I was ever going to have any hope of moving on with my personal life.

It had been more than a year since I had written. Was the skeleton in the basement an excuse? Probably. It's pathetic how little we are willing to know of ourselves, isn't it? His letter back surprised me. In several ways. Surprisingly, Matt writes well. He is not the kind of person you would expect that from. And the letter's contents were surprising too.

Dear D. D.,
Your letter about the skeleton in your cave in Terrassée stopped me in my tracks. I think I must tell you now that I was very much in love all the time that I was living in your house in Terrassée, but there is no real cause for you to be jealous. I was in love with another man who just happened to be a ghost. You will certainly think me pretty crazy when you read this, but I think you should know. Because almost certainly the body in the basement beneath your living room must be that of the man I came to know while I was working there.

It began in the middle of a night, not long before you became so interested in me. Early on, one might say. You will remember that when I came to Terrassée I was delivered there by a friend, who was going on to the south of France, and then into Spain, Alan Dundy. During a night after I had only been in the house a few weeks, I heard steps coming up the staircase. My immediate thought was that Alan had returned from Spain and had gotten a key to the house from the American down the street whom he had met. Funny, isn't it, how the brain works? In a flash I tallied up that it was Alan. He had met Fred down the street while he was here. He knew Fred had a key. It all made sense. Everything must fit into what we think of as possible . . . except it wasn't Alan. The steps stopped when I called out "Alan?".

I turned on the nightstand light and got up and went out into the hallway. I turned on the stairwell light, and there was no one there. I went downstairs and checked the front door. It was firmly locked. There was no one there.

I wasn't frightened. I had no explanation, and yet it didn't seem very important. I went back to bed and to sleep immediately.

I've read that people who have encountered ghosts did not find it terrifying. The famous sighting of Marie Antoinette in the Gardens of Versailles by the two English ladies in the 1930s was like this. She simply passed in the dusk, all in white, and they said "Bonsoir." Only after she had passed did they think that her pannier skirts and powdered hair made it impossible for her to be someone alive in 1933.

I felt the presence of the man near me after that. Do you remember the two small porcelain heads on the dressing table in my bedroom? The Pink bedroom. They always stood at the far corners of the dressing table at either side of the mirror in the center. I entered the room one afternoon . . . and they were together in the center of the dressing table, their lips touching. I knew it was a signal.

I felt him near me. He only touched me once. In the night. If I hadn't been a silly goose and cried out I'm sure I would have felt him more. Perhaps he would have kissed me, as the figurines had kissed on the dressing table. Isn't it curious that my first experience with falling in love with another man should have been with a ghost?

I used to imagine that he would come to me in the night. I created a person in mind. Dark hair. Tight-muscled body. I imagined him between my legs. I tell you all this, D. D., because it will explain a lot about me never being available emotionally to you. I was already taken.

I didn't really want you to come down from Paris and spend the weekend because I wanted to be alone with him. Curious, isn't it? I'm intelligent enough to realize that perhaps it wasn't that I wanted to be alone with my ghost but that I wanted to be alone with the idea that I was interested in other men. I have pondered this very much, and that is why your letter so startled me. There really had been an Alain! I called my ghost love Alain, that's how crazy it had gotten. But now that I know someone was buried in the foundation of the house, that question has been cleared up. He actually did exist once. But I wonder . . . when?

I did see him. Just once. I came into my bedroom at the end of the day and he was there, standing by the bed. He was wearing a white shirt. A shirt with full sleeves and open at the neck. I think he was wearing dark pants. He had long dark hair down to his shoulders, and he was clean shaven. Do you know the actor Sami Frey? Like that. The prototypical romantic hero, exactly the kind of lover anyone would dream of. I looked directly into his very dark eyes, and then he faded. I realized that he had made an enormous effort to appear to me. I don't know how I know this, but I do. Those noncorporeal beings that for some reason are about us can be seen, but the effort must be theirs. Like street people, they never wander far from where their territory has been marked out for them.

So now you perhaps understand why I didn't welcome your presence in Terrassée; did not really want to go to Paris although the work on the house was finished, and it was evident that I had to progress with my life and leave Alain in Terrassée.

Do you remember the day we were leaving for Paris? It was a Sunday. You were going to ride up with your friends, the Panaguas. And shortly before they were to arrive, I was showering and fell out of the tub, tearing the towel rack on the wall out of its moorings as I fell. But I didn't fall. I was pushed. You know how several of your women guests fell or slipped on the stairs that summer? I'm sure it was Alain, who most likely did not like having women around. And he certainly didn't want me to leave. Perhaps he hoped I'd kill myself and be able to join him forever in the house in Terrassée.

I somehow got some shorts on and crawled down to the kitchen where your house guest Anita Something-or-other was putting an icepack on my leg when you walked in. You had just been in the bathroom and seen the water all over the floor and the towel rack torn out. When you entered the kitchen you looked at me not with a look of sympathy but with a look of scorn. I said, "I know, I know. Nothing is by chance." Which, I'm certain, you interpreted as meaning I did not want to go with you to Paris and was willing to break a leg to avoid it. And what I really meant was that Alain was willing to go to any length to keep me there.

You had a doctor there in minutes, even though it was Sunday, and he quickly determined that I hadn't broken my leg. You helped me to dress and sent me off with the Panaguas when they arrived, while Anita and you followed on the train.

Which brings me to the last installment of the drama of Matt. We both have had some getting-over-things to do. You had to get over me, which was always so mysterious to me, as I don't consider myself someone so appealing that anyone would have trouble forgetting me. And I had to get over Alain. And I guess get over being involved with women. Right now, I'm living with a very nice and very handsome ex-priest here in Lake Forest. His name is Dan. I guess I just never realized that one could fall in love with another man and have a domestic relationship like we have. It's very comforting, and I like it very much. My parents have had surprisingly little trouble adjusting to it, although my sisters-in-law obviously think that Dan is wasted on me and should have married one of them.

But not a day goes by, or should I say night, when as I'm drifting off to sleep I don't think of Alain wandering about the old stone house in Terrassée waiting for someone to come rescue him. What do you do with a ghost, D. D.?

I hope you do some sleuthing and find out more about the mysterious stranger on your premises. Do you think such a thing is possible? Perhaps if you find out who my ghost lover was you can have him buried with a headstone somewhere. Maybe that is what keeps ghosts forever haunting this world. They have to be recognized and allowed to go on with their passage to another world. Is this all much too spiritual coming from matter-of-fact, wallpaper-scraping Matt?

I don't think I can sign this letter "sincerely with love." That is a word that neither of us bandy about. But I can easily sign off saying,


Much affection,
Matt


I finished this letter with a great deal to think about. Others have reported ghost sightings in the old house in Terrassée, but I had never heard anything, seen anything, sensed anything. I am not that kind of person. A ghost would not call itself to my attention. I have other things on my mind.

My niece, while sitting on the toilet under the old stairs that turn up to the second floor, reported that footsteps passed upwardly over her head and yet, when she returned to the kitchen, everyone in the household was there.

And then there were two instances of females falling down those stairs. Were they pushed by ghostly hands? At any rate, I now have enough banisters and supporting ropes on the walls that it is like clambering into the crow's nest of a sailing ship.

So what am I supposed to do? I thought as I lay Matt's letter down on my desk. Matt was the key to something. He had dreamed of a woman and a man who seem to have been the first Countess and her lover. Not her husband. Women are rarely so distressed about a husband. And now a handsome young man's ghost wanders about in this house. The first Countess would seem to be the key figure in leading to my ghost. But I have always disliked anything paranormal. And why do I care?

I have always disdained mystery novels because I don't find distraction distracting. My interest is to learn about this life we are leading, and mystery novels never have any relationship to this mysterious murk that we are fumbling and fingering our way through. Life is not like a mystery novel. There is nothing to learn in a book of that kind.

But I do discern traces of destiny unfolding about us if we learn to keep our eyes open. So, evidently, the skeleton and the Countess have to do with my unfolding destiny. And that is how I must interpret the events that followed: my encounter with the mayor in the street in front of the boulangerie, and then seeing the Comtesse for only a moment or two at the Panaguas' annual summer garden party.

# Chapter 5
## The Encounters

There are supposedly a thousand people in Terrassée. I have always said that I have only seen thirty of them in my more than twenty years in the town. I see the butcher and his wife (what is it about butchers that they always seem so meaty? Our butcher, although a young man, looks as though he would only be truly comfortable in refrigeration). And I see the baker regularly, actually his wife, Mme. Cerisier. I have never seen her husband as he is up early and always buried in the bowels of his establishment. I see the two old ladies who live on the corner and are often seated on their stoop. I understand they are mother and daughter, but it would be difficult to ascertain which is which. The bedizened and painted blonde, who is the spouse of the electrician and supervises a shop full of dizzyingly priced electric irons and hair dryers, I also see behind her window. And I see her husband at the wheel of his truck.

The only competitor for chic of the electrical shop blonde is the wife of the owner of the hotel, who is equally blonde and painted and bejeweled and frocked but manages somehow to not seem at all sexually available. There is a feeling that she longs to go to her room and strip off the war paint when one encounters her at the hotel. Her husband, the chef, makes an appearance at the end of the meal. The last time I saw him he was very solicitous of my health. I wonder if I'm aging more rapidly than I think I am.

And then there is the man at the garage, the handsomest man in Terrassée. A young man who has just moved here from nearby St. Marc. The men age rapidly here. In the two years he has been in Terrassée, the bloom is already beginning to fade. Taller than most Frenchmen, he has fine brown eyes, but his features and body are thickening. His pretty young wife behind the cash register does not seem to be fading as rapidly. They have no children yet.

And who else? There is Madame Trian, who looks after my house when I'm not here. Perky, bossy, blonde. And her lumbering husband, who probably takes a lot of bossing around to keep him in motion. And there is the man who runs the café nearest me in the little place. And there are the taxi driver and his wife and son and the son's new wife. Where did she come from anyway? She is not a Terrassée girl, and the son never leaves town. Perhaps she was a passenger. Perhaps it was an arranged marriage (the kind they make in Pakistan).

So what does that add up to? I could add a few more. The man who delivers fuel and wood once a year. And there are perhaps a half-dozen other foreigners who are here some of the year. Plus some old ladies on bicycles I crisscross when I go to the bakery or the grocery. And I forgot the glowering proprietress of the grocery store, whom I know has a husband and son. The husband I don't remember ever seeing, the son only when he was about two. Now I hear him practicing drums over his mother's head, dreaming vainly of escaping Terrassée, I'm sure. Soon he will be stocking shelves. But truly, that's about it. Which makes my running into the mayor, Maitre Hibou, in front of the boulangerie the other day, after I received Matt's surprising letter, something of a real occurrence.

Hibou means "owl" and the good Maitre bears some resemblance to an owl with his perpetually surprised look behind his glasses. He is, in fact, quite an elegant and learned man, one of the last students at the abbey school in our village before it closed at the time of World War Two. I actually find him rather good-looking, which the villagers would scoff at since they see him as the rather self-effacing and ineffective son of his father, also a lawyer here and a former mayor and a quite dynamic personage, evidently. The Hibous are a very old family in this town. Gentry, I suppose, but at the least important level since they were never major land owners. Maitre Hibou always treats me with respect, probably because I bought my house through him and he has subsequently been the notary for the sale of a good number of other houses here to foreigners. I had very little to do with this, but I garner the credit. And I speak French efficiently, which most French people find amazing. When they hear an American speaking French it is with much the same look they might direct toward a talking dog. At first they cannot understand you because they can't imagine you are, in fact, speaking their language. And then there is a kind of wondrous expression when they speak back, and you respond. For them, it is near miraculous. And their highest compliment is when they say, "And you don't have an American accent. More English."

Maitre Hibou had that slightly wondering expression of his when we met and I asked him if he knew anything about the history of my house. He said, "I know in my mother's day there was a kind of girls' school for the local girls in that house. The Comtesse de Cazas of that time conducted it. I don't know what, but I think the de Cazas family always had something to do with that building. At least from the time that they were the de Cazas family. You know that their title is relatively recent. My own family, the Hibous, have been in Terrassée as notaries and lawyers for well over two centuries. The de Cazas were farmers, and I don't think anyone knows much about them before 1800. My father told me that.

"At any rate, I remember my mother telling me that she learned to sew and cook at that school. And when the Comtesse left the room, the girls got up on the table and danced. You should talk to Mademoiselle Cortelage. She was at the school at about the same time as my mother, I believe."

Mademoiselle Cortelage was the guide at the abbey. Her father had been the jeweler in Terrassée, and her brother still ran the little shop on the place near me when I first came to Terrassée. Now he has closed up the windows with false stone and made the shop into his living room. He keeps potted plants in the passageway beside the house and puts them out in front to take the sunlight on days that are not overcast. It is very French that the somewhat stunted plants being raised in shadowy light are given limited amounts of time in the sun when there is some.

One of my neighbors told me that they wouldn't allow their child to have a dog or cat, but they let her have a rabbit. "You cannot imagine the amount of lettuce leaves that rabbit eats." Later they killed the rabbit and ate it. I asked the little girl if she had eaten the rabbit too. She called him Bibou. "Oh, yes, Bibou was very good," she added. I like France, and there is much to admire in the French, but sometimes they break my heart. I have never had a French lover and probably couldn't survive it.

Mademoiselle Cortelage's father was also the local photographer as well as the jeweler. She followed in his footsteps in the recording of village life but did not have his feeling for posing the models or capturing the moment. His photographs have been collected by one of the other foreigners here in the village and a book was published. I should add that it is very unusual for a woman over thirty to be called Mademoiselle. Madame is as much an indication of respect as marital status in France. The only other instance I know of this is the Grand Mademoiselle, the daughter of Gaston of France. She was the niece of Louis the Thirteenth, the only cousin of Louis the Fourteenth, and a big woman and big troublemaker all of her life. Although she had a number of lovers, there was something manly about her and she always had her following.      Mademoiselle Cortelage had something of the same character. I had frequently seen her sitting in her chair knitting at the door to the abbey, awaiting the few and far between visitors. The only time we had spoken was when I visited the abbey when I first came to Terrassée. That is quite some time ago. Now I will have to speak to her again.

"The Comtesse de Cazas of that time was Nathalie's grandmother," Maitre Hibou said. He used the present Comtesse's given name, as he knew we both knew her well enough to be on first name terms. This is the sort of instinctive knowledge one acquires in France. No one had told him. He had never been present when the Comtesse and I had had lunch together, but somehow he knew. This kind of thing is always interesting to me. He added, "I have never been in your house." Amazingly enough, this was true. He supervised the sale of it to me without ever setting foot in it, but then, why should he? Maitre Hibou continued, "But it is old. Certainly those dwellings were built about 1600. That is the site of the old chateau of Terrassée, which was destroyed by the Danes in the eleventh century."

"About the time the abbey was founded," I said.

"Exactly. You know that the Vikings were coming up the rivers and sweeping across the countryside often in those days. And the Danes also. I don't know if what they called the Danes actually came from Denmark," Maitre Hibou said. This was a subject he was warming to. "There are fragments of the old chateau in the houses around you. Your neighbor, Monsieur Lewis (a gentleman who lives to the left of my house and who is in no way anything but French but has an English name. It is pronounced 'Luh-vees' in French) has the remains of an old tower staircase going down into his cave. There is a window with an iron grille on it in that staircase which is completely underground. The entire level of where your house stands must once have been much lower. I imagine that after the chateau was destroyed, they must have built on top of the remains. There are small windows in the house of Monsieur Lewis, as well as some of the houses across the street from his. I think they are windows from the chateau that were reused."

"Was there ever an old graveyard there, do you think?" I asked him. We had been standing quite awhile in front of the boulangerie, but Maitre Hibou didn't seem to mind.

"Why do you ask that?" he said.

"Oh, I ran across a large stone in my garden while I was redoing it," I lied. "Something like the stones they found when they built the mairie back at the turn of the century."

"That was a Roman cemetery under the mairie," he said. "Do you think you have a Roman tomb in your garden?"

"I decided it was more likely a cistern cover," I said. "But it's very large."

"That could be interesting to uncover," he replied.

"It would be very difficult to move. I can't imagine how they put it there in the first place," I said.

"Oh, they had ways of moving things and building things we know nothing about today," Maitre said. "I have a history of the abbey that was written by the Comte de Cazas, Bertrand, Nathalie's brother. I can lend it to you. I have it in my office."

"Perhaps I could stop by and pick it up this afternoon," I suggested. And it was agreed I would do that, and I did.

As I was returning home, Mademoiselle Cortelage was coming out of the abbey gates. I greeted her and told her I had just been talking to Maitre Hibou about the fact that his mother had attended a homemaking school in my house at the same time as Mademoiselle Cortelage.

"She was much older than I am," Mademoiselle said. She is a large dark-haired woman with a jolly manner masking a personality that can in no way be toyed with. Her fragile-looking brother resembles her not at all. She is probably the one who looks like her father.

"She was Mademoiselle Flambeau. Pretty but something of a cow. Not intelligent. We all thought she was inordinately lucky to marry Jean Hibou's father. She was the undertaker's daughter. There was always something dead about her. Do you know what I mean?"

I assured her that I knew exactly what she meant. And I did. Mademoiselle Cortelage was nothing if she wasn't plainspoken.

I told her that Maitre Hibou had said he had never been in my house. "I was in there many times." I was unlocking my door as she said this. "I haven't been in it for many years. I'll come in with you. I'd like to see it again."

I demurred and said I didn't want to keep her from her lunch. "Oh, that doesn't matter," she said and almost pushed me aside as she entered the hallway. "You've made it look very nice," she said. "Not French, but nice."

I, of course, thought I had made my house into the quintessential French country house of the nineteenth century. I did not hear this news with great pleasure.

"This is where we had our classes," she said entering the living room. "Lavender is a very unusual color for a salon," she remarked, looking about.

"Catherine the Empress of Russia had lavender rooms," I offered.

"She was, of course, an Empress," Mademoiselle said. I was beginning to like her very much.

Passing into the kitchen she said, "This is where the Comtesse taught us dancing."

"Maitre Hibou said his mother remembered dancing on the table," I remarked.

"I can't imagine that. She was not a wild kind of girl at all. Perhaps she did. She had nice legs and may have wanted to show them off to us other girls," Mademoiselle said.

She passed out of the kitchen after looking about. I could tell that she thought my fantasy of French country living was amusing. In the garden she indicated the end of the walk and said, "The privies were there. And there was a stable where you have the rest of the garden. I think in early times people must have come in through there. This was once an inn, you know." She gestured to a section of the back wall that was not of the same stone as the rest of the wall. She looked up. "See that little bell up there? Your garden door was the entrance at one time. We never used this room," she stated, nodding toward my green dining room as we went back into the house into the main hallway. "I think someone lived there. I think there were still people living upstairs too."

"Did you ever go upstairs?" I asked.

"No. No one ever did. The Comtesse never did and wouldn't allow any of us to go up there. I think she was afraid to, although she said it was because she had a bad leg. I never noticed that her bad leg gave her any trouble when she was climbing into her carriage. I remember so well that they always came sweeping in from Le Rivage in that big black carriage, and the coachman just whirled across the intersection without looking either way. There were no cars at that time, or very few, but even so, there might have been someone on a bicycle. They wouldn't have cared. She was always in black, with a black bonnet with jet on it so it glittered, and she sat up very straight. I always thought the arrogance was hers. The Comte never made much of a fuss about anything. In they would come, and then descend in front of the church and go down to the aisle to their places in the front row as if it was their church."

"Did you know the present Countess?" I asked her. I didn't ask her to sit down. I know she didn't want to go into the living room and sit down. That would have been a real visit. Another one of those things you come to know in France.

"She wasn't even born then. Her father was still a very young man. A boy, really. This was before the world war. The big one in 1914." I would have loved to know how she referred to the second one. "The unfortunate war? The bothersome war?" No one in Terrassée ever mentioned the 1940 to 1945 period. It was taboo.

—

She glanced up the old wooden staircase. "I remember that the Comtesse never wanted to go up the stairs because I thought she was frightened of going up there. And she was never afraid of anything. I guess I remember it because it was so unusual. But now I must be going and feed my little doggie."

I opened the door. "Perhaps you would come back and have tea with me sometime," I said.

"I would be delighted to," she replied, her bulk filling the doorway. "But, of course, I do not have much to tell about Terrassée. My father came here as a young man to open his shop, so we are newcomers to this town." She looked across the street at the abbey. "I saw my first motion picture there in the Grande Manège, the large exercise building for the horses. The American soldiers brought films with them when they were here during the war, and they showed them to us children in the rear of the abbey. It was very exciting for us." She turned to look at me. "I have always liked Americans," she added and left with no other words.

Let's admit it. Matt's letter had been disturbing. And the fact that everyone I was encountering was source material was even more disconcerting. This seemed much too coincidental. I may like to explore, but there's a limit . . . one I obviously hadn't reached yet.

That afternoon I bicycled over to Maitre Hibou's office and collected the manuscript he had. It had been typed and copied badly. I put it on my desk when I returned home.

In the evening at the Panaguas' garden party I wore white. I always wear white in warm weather. It makes whatever skin tones I have look fresher. Through the mob that always attends these parties and always says the same things I saw the Comtesse's lipstick gleaming. What is that red? Fire and Ice by Revlon? With her white hair and pale face it certainly makes a statement. When she came up to me I noticed for the first time that her teeth are not good. Not neglected. Just not good. And that rather endeared her to me. It linked her to the Empress Josephine, who never opened her lips when she smiled. Nowadays, everyone has perfect teeth. Even me. It's such a bore. Bad teeth guarantee a period look.

"I remembered your question about the color of the library walls and mentioned it to my nephew after you had left the other day. He reminded me that the old original library was where his bedroom now is, not where the old staircase was. My grandfather had an office just beyond that room, and I was often there, but the other rooms were his bedroom and that of my grandmother. My nephew told me that when he removed the paper of that room before repapering, that the wall had been red originally. The wallpaper was gone but the old paper of that period was thin and the dyes were very different. They stained much more. He said the plaster had quite a dark red tint from the wallpaper that had been on it. I don't know why I thought it was green. It must have been in my time. Your question was so curious I long to know why you asked it," she said.

I lied. "It's quite simple actually. I have been thinking of redecorating my salon and thought I might change it to red. Dark red. The editor of Vogue for many years, Diana Vreeland, had a red living room."

"How curious," the Comtesse said and left it at that. "But," she went on, "your question prompted me to dig through an old chest I have full of family documents and things. It's a chest that looks like a baby coffin. We always called it that. I keep it upstairs. I'm not fond of looking at it. I don't know what I thought I would find. Perhaps a sketch or something of the old room. I did run across a batch of letters in a smaller box. The bronze plaque on the top reads, 'Mathilde de Cazas,' which is a name I'm unfamiliar with. I just glanced at them, but they're very bold. The dates go back to the 1830s. My eyes aren't good enough to struggle with them, but I thought you might find them interesting."

I said that I would love to see them, enthusiastic as I was about French history! After the party when we had bid our adieux to Ralph and Inez, I accompanied her to her car. She had brought the box with her, knowing I would undoubtedly be at the party. The box was in an orange and brown Hermès shopping bag. Evidently, the Comtesse was far from running out of funds. Or perhaps that was what she wished me to think. I was very eager to take the box home and look at the letters, but I forced myself to only open the lid and inspect the letters inside, most of them neatly tied up in very fragile ribbon except for the few that the Comtesse had pulled out to look at.

—

I would look at them tomorrow, I told myself, and went up the old wooden staircase to my room. There were no indications of ghosts about, nor were there any during the night.

25

## Chapter 6
## The Box of Letters

I was very excited the next morning, although I did not rise any earlier than I usually do. I sleep until nine o'clock every morning. When I was an editor at Vogue, I never appeared in the office before eleven. Which was always fine with Mrs. Vreeland, who never appeared any earlier either. She always said, "Glamour is difficult before eleven. Impossible before ten."

I made myself dress, go out, and buy the Herald Tribune, and read it over toast and tea before I turned my attention to the letter box. I was not going to let my hopes for mystery solving distort my life.

I think the Comtesse must have slipped the letters she had read from the top of the first ribbon-tied stack, as the first one I unfolded appeared to be a letter from the first Comtesse to an aunt Mathilde when she first appeared at the ChateauLe Rivage as a new bride.

The second appeared to be in sequence and was written one month later. I imagine it must have taken about two weeks for letters to pass to the south of the country, and if her aunt answered promptly, another two weeks for the return mail. The Comtesse Catherine had a fine and spidery hand, and she wrote one sentence stacked neatly and tightly against the one above, which made reading difficult. Rather like those handwritten menus one used to see when I first came to France. Even if you were fluent you could barely read them. They must have been the last gasp of this nineteenth-century manner of writing.

Catherine, Comtesse Contant de Cazas

I very carefully untied the first packet on the top in the box, but the old white satin ribbon fell apart under my fingers. The paper of the letters was fragile and broke here and there on the folds, but the silk of the ribbon crumbled as soon as it was touched. I hoped the present Comtesse would understand my desecration of her family documents. She wouldn't, of course, but there was no help for it. Perhaps I could just slip the others from their tethering in the other packets. The old Comtesse seemed to have been a woman of refinement and some education, as I read, but I couldn't conjure up a personality. What did she look like? What would I have thought if I had been her, if only for a few minutes?

## Chapter 7
## First Letter from Le Rivage


13 August 1837

My Dear Tante Mathilde,

Please accept my excuses for not writing to you sooner, but there has been so much to do to acclimate myself to this new life that I am now living as the chatelaine of the chateau of Le Rivage.

I, myself, did not clearly understand what my life would be here, lost as I was in the fantasies of any woman about a world in which she will soon be living. Which is not to suggest that the reality is in any way shocking or disagreeable. That it most certainly is not. But since Le Rivage is not just a large building but the center of a very large farm of many hectares with a number of adjoining properties, there is a great deal of work for my husband, and I am determined to make every effort to aid him in his endless labors.

But first of all, let me describe the landscape of this new world. Unlike the landscape that surrounds Aix, where you are now and where I have spent my life until now, here there is green, green, green reaching in every direction. The green and yellow of great fields of grain, just now being gathered in. Here, there are no rocky projections from the earth, there are no distant mountain peaks capped by little villages. Here, the land reaches out in all directions in perfect flatness. Of course, when we go by coach to a nearby town to buy

Mathilde, Comtesse de Cazas. Aunt of Catherine

necessities there are descents to the riverbeds, near to which many of the towns huddle. But these are almost the only examples of descents and ascents. Once the upper levels have been reattained, the coach rolls along very smartly, and soon we are at home again.

As there are in Aix, the country roads are lined with trees to provide shade for the traveler. But in addition, there are large stretches of green forest. Forests that are full of magical glades and trees that reach out for another across the carriage tracks. It is easy to imagine how the writers we have read together, who tell of fairy beings flitting on the tips of their toes through the glens, came to imagine the gossamer creations floating about. I, myself, can well imagine the famed Taglioni on her pointes leaning down from a branch to enchant some handsome rustic workman passing by. *[Marie Taglioni, the famous dancer, who was the first to dance on her toes in ballets created for her like La Sylphide and other romantic period ballets. Her light and ethereal style was much copied by other dancers.]*

Of course, you and I have only dreamed of seeing her dance, but I hope my new husband will take me to Paris to see her float in her unequalled way across the stage of the opera.

As for Le Rivage itself, my husband has only really begun to create the chateau that will someday be the largest and the most important in this region. Certainly the largest that has been built in several centuries. We are not too far from the great chateau of Chambord, which I hope to visit before too long, and Le Rivage will not be the equal of one of these mountainous royal chateaus created to house hundreds of courtiers, but it will be a very handsome modern chateau with large light rooms which you will much enjoy when you come to visit us. This, I hope, will be soon and for a very, very long stay.

The chateau, when completed, will be in the form of a "U," the front side facing the road that passes before our gates, and the two wings running back from this. My husband inherited the two large buildings that form the wings. One had been the home of parents, and probably was built more than one hundred years ago. Perhaps more than one hundred and fifty, in the time of the reign of Louis the Fourteenth. Facing it across a large courtyard is a similar building that was built at the same time to house the many maids and cooks and farmworkers necessary for a property of this size. And I can certainly hazard the guess that stables for horses and cows may very well have been included there at the time it was built. Now, there are large barns built at some distance from the chateau, but they are of more recent date. And certainly there is no shame is occupying buildings which once housed animals. These are strong, stone-built edifices which have already seen many uses and will surely see more.

It is my husband's excellent concept to join these buildings with a large modern building which will contain large reception rooms, which his parents' home sorely lacks. I should say that this is far more than a concept as this building is nearly completed, although still unoccupied as the work of internal plastering and floor installation is being done even as I write this letter.

Monsieur Contant has had the idea of building the new connecting wing with a handsome arched opening completely through the building so that arriving guests can enter with their carriage into the interior courtyard. On either side of this entryway are handsome rooms. Part of my responsibility, as the new chatelaine, will be deciding the use of these rooms. Certainly one will be a large dining room in which one can entertain guests and family, and one should be a library where one can cozily read before the fire during the long winter months here. Although it is very warm now, my husband assures me that there will be many days of rain and overcast skies and that days will be short and dark. I look forward to this. It will be very different from our life in the south where every day was almost always sunny.

On the first floor above the entrance archway will be a very
large room that can be used for a ballroom, with large rooms on
either side. Perhaps one will be my sitting room and the other our
bedroom. At the moment, we are very comfortably ensconced in
what was his parents' bedroom. The furniture is pretty but with the
curves and the light colors of the last century. I do not think it is
suitably large and imposing enough for this new house now being
finished. Oh, how I wish you were with me now to help decide what
the furniture should be like and what colors should be used for the
decoration of these new rooms.

Almost all of the dresses and ornaments from my trousseau
have been worn and much appreciated. The plaid silk dress that I
chose to travel in was an excellent choice on your part. I am foolish
enough to think that it flatters me and the straw bonnet that we had
decorated with matching ribbons looks very pretty with it.

My white eyelet embroidered peignoir has been, perhaps, the
most successful of my entire wardrobe. I wear it each night before
retiring and in the morning when I take my petit dejeuner in my
room. I had doubts as to how well it would survive the packing for
the trip, but your maid packed all my things exceedingly well.

I have not yet attended any evening parties here. That will
commence this autumn when all the local families have returned
from their various visits to their relatives and friends. There are a
number of titled families here whom I am eager to meet and know.
There are also a large number of important personages of the church
in this region as we are not too far from Blois, where there is a large
bishopric. One of the persons assisting the bishop is a distant cousin
of mine, and I will surely write to see if he wishes to pay us a visit
once the new part of the house is prepared for guests.

I know you will want news of Marion. She assures me almost daily that she in no way regrets accompanying me here and, of course, her services to me are invaluable. I do not think I would have found a local woman to serve as my maid who can wash and iron with the refinement of Marian. And her capabilities in dressing my hair are well-known to you. My hair is washed with great regularity at least every two weeks, and whenever possible, we dry it in the sunlight, which gives it the highlights I am so pleased to have. Most days we dress it in a coronet of braids on the top of my head, but when I have had the occasion to dress more formally, she has concocted some delicious loops and curls, decorated with my combs and ribbons, that have been much admired. Marion is extremely adept at copying the pictures that we see in the ladies' newspapers that we have been able to obtain from Paris. We both hope that we shall be able to go to Paris before long. It is only a two-day coach ride from here, assuming that one will spend a night at Orléans or nearby. My husband has had business in Paris several times, but he travels one full day and full night without stop and returns as quickly as possible.

Have I left out anything from this perhaps overly long missive to you, my much-loved aunt? Perhaps I have written at such length to reassure you that I am comfortable and satisfied in my new life as someone's wife. We shared misgivings about a marriage to a man who was unknown to us. There seemed few, if any, viable prospects among the people we knew, and at twenty-six, I could not hope to compete with the fresher and younger demoiselles who were cropping up about the countryside. There, I know you are cringing at what you will call my "frankness." But we were always capable of speaking without subterfuge. Through friends, Monsieur Contant was recommended to us, and although he only paid one visit before our betrothal, I believe our impression of him was accurate, and I have seen nothing to contradict it. He is tall, he is certainly handsome enough to satisfy any woman's taste, and he is in a position to care for his wife in all the ways that are necessary. The difference in our ages is not so great as we once feared. He is youthful and almost boyish at times at forty. And there is, at times, almost something paternal in the attention he pays to me. Insofar as my duties to him as a wife are concerned, he is gentle and understanding and that side of our marriage is eminently satisfactory, as far as I am concerned.

I think I can honestly say that I do not, in fact, see enough of him, since his duties about the estate require much of his time. He is up early and often eats his midday meal in distant parts of his holdings. I occupy myself well planning meals with our cook, whom I have not discussed but who is excellent and very open to my ideas about adding our southern way of cooking to the meals to be eaten here at Le Rivage. And there are the linens and the maids to supervise in the cleaning. I think the women of our household like me and will come to me with their problems and worries, which I am more than happy to discuss with them. There has not been a chatelaine here at Le Rivage for some years, so these are all duties that I think can only improve the life of our household.

Now I have run on far too long and taken up far too many pages. You will think that I have too little to do, but this is not, in fact, the case. It is because of my great love for you that I wish you to know of my life here in all its details. Please believe that I think always of you with great tenderness and affection.

Your niece,
Catherine

**Chapter 8**
**Second Letter from Le Rivage**


20 September 1837
My Dear Tante Mathilde,
Now the harvest season is almost over. This has been an excellent year for the vineyards. It was a dry summer, which is always good for the grapes. Only now is there some rain, which is making it more difficult for the local people who come out from the village to help with the picking, but they are managing well despite the difficulties. This is something we did not see much of in our part of the world, where the farmers raise grapes only for their own little winemaking. Here, there is a very large winepress in one of the outbuildings of Le Rivage, which is kept very busy as the pickers bring the grapes in from the vineyards.

There is a large basket that each picker carries on his or her back. They toss the bunches of grapes over their shoulder, cutting each bunch loose with a small, sharp knife with something of a curve to the blade. Something like the Muslim dagger. When the basket is full, it is carried to a large cart, which is bullock drawn, and the grapes are hauled back to the press.

Do not think that people climb into a vat and march about, as we have seen in Italian etchings. The process is far more modern than that. There is a large stone basin with a large kind of wooden corkscrew suspended above it, holding a wooden platform on its end. A very large beam is at the top of the corkscrew and four men march in a large circle, turning it down upon the grapes. There is an aperture at the side of the stone basin, and the juice from the grapes runs out here and is carried by a stone trough to a large stone cistern sunken in the ground, where the juice is collected and ferments. After a time, it is taken out and poured into wooden barrels and stored in the large caves that are under the chateau where it ages. The local wine is called Gamay, which is not like the wines we are used to in the south. It is lighter and sweeter. I prefer it to the Bordeaux wines that we always served.

It is a pleasure to have the chateau surrounded by the merry grape pickers. They are all very high-spirited, arriving in the bullock carts from Terrassée just as daylight breaks. Some kind of horse drawn cart is also used. I think for the local people the grape harvest is a kind of kermesse. It is an opportunity for them to do something together. There is a great deal of flirting between the young men and women, and I imagine that a great many marriages take place after the harvest where lovers have met.

It has been very quiet at the chateau since my arrival, and all the noise and gaiety make a welcome change. Monsieur Contant informs me that as soon as the harvest is in we will begin to have more social activities. In the winter months, when there is less to do here at the chateau and the farming season is over, evidently people amuse themselves by giving parties and balls. Some of these are at quite a distance so that it is necessary to stay for several days. Hopefully, I will have the opportunity to wear some of the beautiful dresses that were prepared for my trousseau. I particularly wish to wear the green satin dress I was married in, as I think the color suits me very well.

I would like your opinion, dear Aunt, on a subject that I wouldn't say worries me, but perhaps I could say perplexes me. Monsieur Contant has expressed a desire to share my title with me. He would like to be known as the Comte Contant de Cazas. I assured him that I was perfectly willing to be known as Madame Contant. I know it is not customary for the male in a marriage partnership to take his wife's title. His argument is that our son will take the title Comte de Cazas, and he would like him to bear the name Contant also. And if his son is to have that title, why shouldn't he bear it now? As you well know, all this is of no interest to me. Although our family's title is a true title and was awarded so very long ago in the time of Charles the Seventh, it was only a way of claiming the loyalty of others and avoiding revolutions. Which seems quite clear, in this year of 1837, did not work any too well in the last century.

I wish Monsieur Contant to be happy, and since there are very few titles in this region, I don't think it makes very much difference. I would hope that we are both modern women and have no feeling that a title is any kind of assurance that one is a kinder or more generous or more interesting person for laying claim to one.

Speaking of modern women, did I mention that Mme. Dudevant, the writer who uses George Sand for her pen name, resides at not too far a distance from Le Rivage? I'm sure someone like myself would be of no interest to her, but I would like so very much to visit her chateau at Nohant, which lies to the south of us here. I'm sure you know that her grandmother was a lady-in-waiting to Marie Antoinette, and that her great-grandfather was the Maréchal de Saxe, and that her great-great-grandfather was the king of Poland. And that her grandfather on her mother's side sold birds along the Seine in Paris. She claims, quite without embarrassment, that she is descended from the kings of Poland and the people of Paris. She also rises above the fact that almost none of her ancestors ever bothered to marry one another. I find these kinds of attitudes very refreshing. I know that it shocks you to have me write this.

I look forward with great interest to your reply to this letter, my very, very dear aunt. Your advice is always of the wisest variety. The only thing that would complete my happiness would be if you were to come for a very long visit. Or come here to live with us. Is that such an extraordinary idea?

I remain with a love that is not to be questioned,
Your niece,
Catherine

**Chapter 9**
**Third Letter from Le Rivage**


27 October 1837

My Dear Tante Mathilde,

Now it becomes chill and cold here in this damp valley between the Loire and Cher rivers. You and I have only experienced this weather in the month of January in the sunnier world that we inhabited when we were together. Even though this part of the world is famous for its gentle weather, the days have become short and skies more often gray than not. I am sure that soon this will all become normal to me.

Our big excitement since I wrote you last has been a shooting party organized by Monsieur Contant, or as you advised me to call him in your last letter, my husband the Count. I know that I will always think you are writing about my father, rather than my husband when you use the title until I get more used to it. As with the skies and the cold winds, I am sure that I will become accustomed to it given more time.

Did I tell you that Le Rivage has a very large pond on its property? Almost a lake. In the summer when I arrived, it was low and almost invisible in its reeds, but now with the almost daily rains we have had, it is full to the brim and easily accommodates a good many boats. The ducks in their passage stop at this pond, which is possibly where the source of the name of this chateau comes from, and it is the custom for the friends of my husband to assemble here for a few days for a hunt.

We have six couples staying with us, several of them from Blois, and Monsieur and Madame Vernaduchi even traveling from Loches, which is a very long day's coach trip from here. The chateau is overcrowded with people as almost everyone, except some of the single men, arrive with their servants and horses and vehicles and dogs.

In addition, there are some ten local friends of my husband who come from nearby so that they are able to ride to Le Rivage each morning.

I arouse myself even before daylight to see that coffee and food is prepared for the men. They wish to be in their duck blinds before it is fully light. The ducks sweep in with a great flapping of wings and settle on the pond, and then they are set aloft by the clapping of wooden blocks together, and the men fire away. I think it is only their grown-up way of enjoying the same pleasures as they enjoyed as children on Bastille Day, with all the fireworks, the cracking and the popping replicating all the miniature explosions men seem to enjoy so much.

I come out at midday with a wagon of food with some of the men from the chateau. I have a horse that I have been trying to ride every day, but she is skittish, and I do not like her half as well as my Belle. It is strange, isn't it, that we can miss animals so much, sometimes even more than people? I know Belle is in good hands with my brother, but even so, there are many times that I wish that she were here with me. My new horse's name is Trompette, which I would like to change, but evidently that is not permissible as she is a finely bred horse and the name is registered somewhere with someone. In any case, Trompette and I turn and weave about a great deal as we cross the fields with the wagon lumbering behind us.

I bring several of the maids from the chateau with us to help me serve. There is one I particularly like named Minette whom, I think, may become a personal maid for me. Marion speaks a great deal about returning to the south, and I certainly do not want her to remain here against her wishes. I believe she wishes to marry Robert, who has been serving in your kitchen. Perhaps she believed that she might find a worthier husband here, but that has not arrived on her horizon. When Marion was ill with a cold I had Minette help me with my hair, and she was very capable. I think she has a knack for it.

And so we have strayed from ducks to my hair with my scarcely noticing it. The duck hunting only lasts for three days as the ducks have the good sense to depart without overstaying their welcome and before they are entirely decimated.

Each night I must see that a very large dinner is prepared as we have some twenty people to sit down together. And that is not even to speak of the mob that is eating in the kitchen. Cook has been a saint and is holding up very well. For the last evening, I implored my husband to organize a small ball in our new large and grand room that sits astride the carriage entrance, and it was very much a success. Some of the people from Terrassée were invited . . . the mayor, the doctor, some of the professors from the abbey. Even the director of the abbey consented to come. He is a priest and celebrated scholar but seemed to have a very enjoyable time surrounded by flowing wine and pretty women.

My only disappointment was that I planned to wear the pink damask gown that was made for dancing, but when I showed it to my husband, he thought it showed off too much of my shoulders. "The people around here are not used to seeing so much of a woman's body," he said, "and besides, the weather is too cold for you to uncover so much of yourself." I know you will laugh at that as you must be thinking of the décolletage of Madame LaVigne, who always showed off so much of her body even when it was long past its delectable stages. He is right, though, that the people here are very reserved, almost Protestant in their demeanor. He has been very attentive and affectionate since that evening, however, so I believe he felt my disappointment. Perhaps I will never wear that pink dress at all.

At any rate, we are now well into our autumn season. The maid Minette has promised to teach me how to knit, so I will begin making some garments to keep my husband and myself warm during the winter. You will, fortunately, not need any such garments. In your next letter, please write and tell what the weather is like and particularly describe your flowers.

I remain, as always, a person who holds you in the greatest esteem and has only the most devoted feelings for you.

Your niece,
Catherine

**Chapter 10**
**Fourth Letter from Le Rivage**


30 November 1837

My Dear Tante Mathilde,

I have just discovered something astonishing. My husband has a brother of whom nothing has ever been said, nor have I ever heard him mentioned in front of me. And, of course, I have never seen him. My new maid Minette mentioned him to me quite casually yesterday morning while she was preparing my hair for the day. She said, "All of us here at Le Rivage are so looking forward to the day when the Comtesse will have little children of her own so they can play with all their little cousins." I understood immediately that she was telling me that little cousins existed and knew full well that I was quite unaware of their existence. Minette is not at all stupid.

I then said, quite without any urgency in my voice, "But where are the little cousins? Why do we never see them here at Le Rivage?"

"They are with their father and mother in St. Marc. I think Monsieur (she did not call my husband Monsieur the Count I noticed, though she is always careful to call me Countess) and his brother have an unhappy history of some kind, and they do not see each other. My sister lives next door to Monsieur and Madame Contant in St. Marc, and I have had the pleasure of meeting them and their children."

"How many children are there?" I asked.

"Five," she told me, "and they are all very nice."

"But how old is the eldest?" I asked again.

She said, "About ten, I would imagine. Her name is Estelle. She is a very intelligent little girl and a great assistance to her mother."

"That is a great many children," I said only. "Monsieur and Madame Contant love children and evidently cannot have too many. They love each other, also, which is quite evident." I looked at her in the mirror while she was saying this, and there was not a trace of a smile on her face when she spoke. I said, "I will have to talk to Monsieur the Count (I made a point of saying this to her) and see if we can have them come for a visit. I would love to meet them." I let her leave at this point. I dislike having my maid dress me unless it is absolutely necessary, and I have made a point of having all my daily dresses made with buttons down the front so I can accomplish this by myself.

Clearly, here was something to think about. It is at time like this that I wish you were here to discuss such interesting subjects in person. I lack female friends of my own station here, and I am not about to make the error of confiding in my maid. That is always a mistake.

That evening at our dinner, since we were alone, I asked my husband about his brother. "How did you hear about this?" he asked, not in an alarmed way.

"My maid mentioned it to me quite casually in passing. I suppose she imagined that I was well aware of such a family connection. I understand he has a great many small children."

"Who can remember all those names?" my husband said. "It seems his wife and he wish to use the letters of the alphabet to keep their children in order in their own minds. At the rate they are going, they will easily reach twenty-six before his wife is no longer able to have children."

"But I understand the eldest child is a girl and is called Estelle," I said.

"I don't know anything about that," he answered me. "We have not spoken since the time of marriage."

"Would I be indiscreet if I inquired why?" I asked him.

We had finished our cutlets and had not rung for anyone to come clear the table yet. He told me that his brother, who is younger, was always a rather irresponsible person. He had not done well at the abbey school and had never completed his education there. He had wished to marry one of the maids at the chateau and had been completely forbidden to even think of this by their father, who then had the bad luck to die. Although, as you well know, all property in France must be evenly divided among heirs, their father had stipulated that Jacques, that is the brother's name, was to remain a co-owner of Le Rivage, and the property was not to be sold or divided. My husband explained to me that this is highly questionable as to legality. His brother wished to sell Le Rivage as he has no interest in running it. What has been arranged is that his brother has signed papers agreeing to accept a certain sum annually as his share of the money made in the sale of crops, wine, and other products and animals from the chateau. Because of this, my husband does not wish to see his brother or his family.

Those are all things that no one was informed of at the time of my marriage settlement, and I am not at all sure that it would have made any difference. To be sure, I am well satisfied with my marriage, and my life lacks for nothing. But I had hope that my husband would have been more modern and thought I was quite intelligent enough to understand all this. Whether my uncles would have is quite another story and one that we must leave unexamined.

Please believe, my dear aunt, that I am not telling you this so that you can recount it to Uncle Louis. I would not wish to distress him in any way.

I asked my husband who Madame Jaques Contant was, and he replied rather grumpily, "Sylvie, the maid, of course. He could certainly have had children with her without marrying her, but that is not his way." And he rang for the plates to be cleared.

My new brother-in-law sounds like a not-at-all-bad character to me. I wholeheartedly approve of his marrying his Sylvie, and since his annual income seems to be adequate for his ever-increasing brood, why should he not breed as he pleases? I know that you will find these kinds of ideas rather advanced, but, in truth, where did I get those kinds of idea if not from you?

So there you have it. I have a brother-in-law I most likely will not meet. A sister-in-law that I cannot meet. And a battalion of nephews and nieces I may finally meet in my old age.

———

What is quite clear is that I must get busy and start having some little cousins for these nephews and nieces as I feel quite sure that my husband does not wish to have those children inherit Le Rivage, which is so important to him and so dear to his heart. I cannot say that I love him any more than I did at the time of our marriage. I can see you rolling your eyes to the heavens at such frankness, but I certainly like him better and understand him better. He is a good man and a not unkind man. He has inherited an estate, and his concern during this life is to take care of it well. As the Bible teaches us in the parable of the master who goes away and leaves a talent for each of the three servants to be responsible for, there is the servant who spends it unwisely, there is the servant who buries it, and the servant who invests it and returns it to the master many times increased. I believe my husband wishes to be like the third servant, and when his life is through, have made more from what was given him. I myself would interpret the parable in a more spiritual way and think that the increase should be in the understanding, loving, and forgiving of our fellow man, but then again, I am a woman, not a man. Each sex must approach life in the way that is most natural for them.

But enough of this rattling on. The fire is burning low in the grate, the room becomes cold, and my candle is flickering low, also. My husband has been very understanding about my wanting a fire in my boudoir all day and into the evening, but he does not entirely approve of my sitting up and writing late into the night, even to my dear and beloved aunt.

Since I know that it is important for me to bear children, I should be going to my bed wearing something like my white lace peignoir and with my hair down, but I assure you that it is far too cold here to even dream of such romantic notions. My husband retires before I do after his long day with his farmers as a rule and is asleep when I get there. It is clear that I must start a different kind of routine soon, but perhaps not before spring. I know you will consider this kind of confidence far too outspoken, also, but since we have gotten in the habit of being outspoken with each other, I think it is far too late to bring our exchanges into a more restricted pattern.

As always, I remain your most loving niece,

Catherine

---

A little postscript comes into my mind as I seal this letter. There will soon be a train connection quite near to us in Blois. I have never traveled upon this new invention, nor certainly have you, but perhaps you would be daring enough to try to come visit us at Christmas and for the New Year if it exists by then. I will discuss this with my husband in the morning and add another final note. A very fervent embrace.

## Chapter 11
## Author's Interjection

There are no letters from Catherine, Comtesse Contant de Cazas, for the month of December 1837 and January 1838, which suggests that her request that her aunt visit her at this time was answered affirmatively and Aunt Mathilde spent time at Le Rivage in that period.

Although the young Comtesse discusses train travel in her letter, it would not have been possible at that time, although there must have much discussion of it. The first train was inaugurated between Paris and the suburb of Auxerrois two years later on a commercial basis, although the engineer, Marc Seguin, had built a train connection between Lyon and Saint-Étienne as early as 1826. The connection of cities in France was to be very rapid, and it would certainly have been possible to make the trip to Le Rivage in that way not many years later. Once this happened what would have probably been a one-week trip could have been reduced to two days and perhaps less. The advent of the train was to truly connect the French world in a way it had not been before and changed the texture of that society greatly, particularly in the world of the arts. George Sand frequently refers to the ease of this new kind of travel that allowed her to move back and forth from her literary stardom in Paris to her household in Nohant, south of the chateau of Le Rivage.

Curiously, the young Comtesse does not refer to this visit by her aunt in her subsequent letters, but again she had many reasons to pay close attention to what was currently happening in her life.

---

# Chapter 12
## Lunch with the Comtesse


From D. D. Abercrombie's Journal:

My translating of the letters of the first Comtesse was going slowly, although I was fascinated. I was determined to not do literal translations but to truly do an idiomatic rendering of the Comtesse's neat hand and quite literary style. Perhaps I am too influenced by Jane Austen, of whom I am a great fan. I rather imagined the Comtesse's experiences as being tantamount to the country world of Jane Austen. Perhaps I was bringing too much of a free-wheeling twentieth-century mind-set to my enterprise. I was truly trying not to anticipate a melodrama that I had created in my head in advance of real information. But there was another aspect to this adventure I couldn't ignore. There was something unusual about the placing in my hands of information that I had no right to expect to find.

Perhaps the countryside that circled Terrassée was not at all the same kind of contained, regulated world in which Jane Austen had lived. France had, after all, quite a different history from that of England, and most importantly, the English had not had a revolution. In the Comtesse's letters that I had translated so far, there was a sense of a world that was trying to put itself back together in a way that both resembled the eighteenth century, as well as the more secure and settled English world that the French have always admired.

At least these thoughts were entering my mind when the present Comtesse called. Furthermore, it was not to invite me to a large party, or even lunch, at her home at the restored farmhouse. She wished to invite me to a lunch with her at the Toque Blanche, the best restaurant in nearby Saint Marc. Her son was visiting, and she thought he would enjoy meeting me. I was puzzled by this invitation and wondered what the Comtesse had up her sleeve. This certainly was not some attempt at matchmaking. I am much more the Comtesse's age than I could possibly be her son's. Did the Comtesse herself have romantic inclinations toward me? I was of a certain age and had no man in my life. Perhaps she thought I was a lesbian. A lipstick lesbian, one would hope. I've never been criticized for being mannish, and I hate horses. I dismissed that idea also.

Whatever it was, the Comtesse was rolling out her heavy guns. No French person invites you to lunch at an expensive restaurant simply for the pleasure of your company. Everything in France, from the couture to the hairdressing to the restaurants, is designed as a tool in the endless adventure of getting something you want. And that something will always involve things and/or money. Or the preservation of a reputation, the loss of which might keep you from getting things and/or money.

I assured the Comtesse that I would love to come to lunch at La Toque Blanche the following day, Thursday, and added that 12:30 would be ideal, saying that wasn't it nice that it wasn't market day and parking would be easy.

—

48

The next day I drove the five minutes to Saint Marc and easily found a spot to park across the street from the restaurant. It's one that I know well. Two sisters and their sister-in-law, always elegantly dressed, are always on hand to greet and seat customers and to take orders. The brother is in the kitchen, and the charming elderly parents are always on hand, hovering in case the children go awry. I imagine this must have been a restaurant founded by them, and they do not wish to see any decline in service or quality. As I entered, I wondered when they had started their restaurant. After the Second World War perhaps? They would be the right age for that. I vaguely considered interviewing them for a fictitious article but put that thought aside as the Comtesse smiled with red, red lips and waved to me from across the room. A rather good-looking man with fair hair in his middle to late thirties was seated beside her. This must be the son, I concluded. He was wearing an open-necked shirt and a leather jacket. This was not someone from Paris.

The Comtesse lost no time in coming to the point. As soon as we had ordered she turned to me and said, "Are you finding the letters interesting? I'm so eager to know. And I am so interested as to why you should find our little country world so interesting."

"Nathalie, you know I am an incurable Francophile," I said. "Everything about France interests me. Even as a small child in Ohio, my dream was to speak French and live in France. Et voilà. Here I am, doing exactly that. Do you live near here?" I said, turning to her son.

He smiled. Nathalie answered for him. "He is the master of the stable for Monsieur de Bouillet, Giscard d'Estaing's cousin. The Duc de Bouillet, actually. They have a large stable near Chateauroux. His wife is an American." She added the last as though it was something I could personally be proud of. "It is not far away, but even so, he comes to see me only rarely." This last was added in a flirtatious manner, as though her son was one of her suitors.

He had a handsome face and good hands, the son. But he was obviously not a man who ever made any effort to please. "He very much resembles the portrait of your grandfather you showed me at the chateau," I said to the Comtesse. Now we were both talking about her son as though he was an object that neither of us thought was going to join in the conversation.

"And my great-grandmother too, I understand," said the Comtesse. "My grandmother, who knew him well, always said that she had married my grandfather because she had fallen in love with his father. And they looked so much alike she was delighted to capture his son. I think that I resemble my mother whom, of course, I never knew." One never rambled very far in conversation from the Comtesse herself. She was enjoying her soup. "Oh, but do speak for yourself," I said to her son. What was his name? Had she said Gerard when she introduced him? I certainly couldn't ask him now. I decided to think of him as Gerard and not call him anything.

"Are you happy at the de Bouillets with their horses?" I knew this was a very American way of speaking but decided to give it a try.

"I like it very much," the perhaps-Gerard said. "I am very fortunate to have this kind of work. There are not many of these positions available in France."

"One of my brothers went to school with Gaston de Bouillet," the Comtesse explained. The waiter was clearing our first course dishes.

The Comtesse was not to be deterred. "So what are you finding out about the first Comtesse Contant de Cazas? Was she anything like me?"

"I think she was a woman of very good intelligence. Which is very much like you," I said. I was willing to flatter, and it is always better for one woman to praise another woman's intelligence, rather than her beauty, I have found. And if the Comtesse was secretly yearning for me, this was certainly a compliment that would not lead to later complications. "But I'm not sure of what she looked like. I imagine her with dark hair for some reason. She writes of parting it in the middle. Since she was from the South, I think of her as having dark hair and eyes. I could be completely wrong, however."

"I was blonde when I was young," the Comtesse said.

"Not very blonde," her son broke in.

The Comtesse ignored him. "I have a colored drawing that may be of her. It is of a woman with dark hair and a high comb. No one ever said it was a portrait of the first Countess. She's wearing one of those bigsleeved dresses they wore in the beginning of the nineteenth century."

"Are there buttons down the front?" I asked. "There might very well be. It has a high lace collar as I recall. I'll have to look when I get home. It always hung in the upper hall at La Rivage, and I took it since things are so dilapidated up there. What a curious question. Did someone dream of seeing her?" she said.

I laughed. "Not at all. She mentions in one of her letters that she does not like her maid to dress her and prefers to have buttons down the front of her dress so that she can dress herself."

"Are you sure you didn't dream it?" the Comtesse said, looking at me piercingly with her eyes. Her very blue eyes. His were very dark eyes. Completely different.

"No. No more dreams. And if I do, I promise I will tell you." I looked at the two of them sitting across the table from me. We were all eating our strawberries. I always try to have fruit for dessert in France. Otherwise, one can explode into a many-kilo-ed version of one's former self.

How enigmatic they were to me. And I suppose to themselves as well. Perhaps it is better to live in the American style and have no idea even what your grandparents' names were or where they came from. There was history behind these people. A history they themselves were only vaguely aware of, but it made them profoundly uneasy to have someone examining it.

As we rose from the table, the Comtesse said to me, "Perhaps you should visit the village church, which is quite near you. You're not Catholic, are you? No one in the United States is. There is a chapel dedicated to Saint Catherine that the first Countess gave to the church. Perhaps there is something there. I don't go to church myself, so I haven't seen it for years. But it could be interesting.

"And I think there is a dedication to the first Count in the abbey chapel somewhere, also. I remember being shown it on one of the pillars. I cannot imagine what it was for, as they are both buried in the Terrassée cemetery. I don't think anyone is buried in the chapel."

She turned to look at me again with that sharp-eyed look of hers. "I'm flattered that you are so interested in our family history. Perhaps you will write something about us."

"I cannot write at all," I said. "I am a hopeless writer. But I am taking notes, and I would be delighted to go over them with you someday. I have always found history fascinating, and don't you think that we are all the result of generations of people who were happy, unhappy, jealous, proud— all of those things? Our personal psychology could have come down to us from an ancestor who was jealous of her sister. And every generation only compounds and deals with those feelings as they are passed down. I think that is what psychology is about. It's not just your parents, it's the whole tribe back and back and back." This was a long speech for me, and I could tell the Comtesse was lost, and her son quite clearly was longing to get back to his horses. Or Madame de Bouillet or something. We shook hands and bid each other adieu. I was eager to get back to Terrassée and go visit the village church and the abbey chapel if they were open.

## Chapter 13
## The Chapel of Saint Catherine

As soon as I had parked the car I walked down the Passage du Salut to the entrance of the village church in Terrassée. Climbing the steps I found the door open. Walking down the aisle on the right I quickly found the chapel that had been given to the church by the first Comtesse. It was essentially an alcove of stone with a large painting on the front wall. A low railing and kneeling ledge ran in front of this painting at a distance of about two feet from it, and against the back wall was a low-backed bench with an ornately carved frame and arms, covered in what was now extremely fatigued red leather. The large window on the back wall was a mid-Victorian fantasy of Saint Catherine done in the vivid glass of that period and a host of more-Gothic-than-Gothic curlicues and squiggles framing it. Saint Catherine could have been any lovely saint in the window depiction.

The painting was something else. In the painting, Saint Catherine stood tall and slender on the right and seemed to be already in heaven. An angel, who seemed to be male, was greeting her on the left surrounded by cherubim and seraphim. It was actually not a bad painting. I wondered if the Comtesse herself had been the subject for the figure of the saint. Upon careful inspection, the painting was badly in need of repair. There were many small cracks and some flaking here and there, revealing the bare canvas underneath. This dark little village church was surely not the best environment for a painting of . . . how many years? The painting wasn't dated, but a plaque beside it read that the chapel had been dedicated in 1841. I imagined that it wouldn't have been done so without the painting being in place. The plaque read that the chapel had been offered by the very kind and generous Comtesse Catherine Contant de Cazas.

I stepped back and tried to get some feeling for what the chapel must have been like at the time of its creation. Certainly the carved wood and black leather and close-to-life-size painting must have been startling and luxurious in this very plain little stone church. And even now, in its dilapidated state, there were still prayers being said in it, as the faded flowers in brackish water in the glass vase that stood on the railing testified.

I went in and knelt myself, studying the painting as I placed my folded hands under my chin. The saint had dark hair parted in the middle. Her eyes were downcast so the eye color wasn't apparent, but her fine profile seems to be that of a real model, if not the Comtesse herself. The nose was prominent with a slight arch, which truly could not be called classic. The saint also had a very nice bosom, but that could have been simply a Victorian convention.

Rising from my knees, I went to the stained glass window again, and this time, I noticed that it was dated in the lower left corner. It read 1848. So the window was put in place some seven years after the chapel had been created. Had it been ordered and just took a very long time to be finished? Or perhaps the Comtesse had come into some money and decided to enhance her chapel even further. How would any of these questions ever be answered? I felt as though I was only uncovering more questions all the time and finding very few answers to my romantic and dramatic scenario.

I proceeded to the abbey to see if I could find a commemorative plaque there regarding the Count.

Although the gate to the abbey was open, Our Lady of the Snows was closed. Another day I would have to take the tour, and then quiz Mademoiselle Cortelage to see if she had any information that might be useful.

Once at home, I decided to do some investigating in the cemetery the next morning. I still didn't know how old the first Comtesse was when she died. She obviously had had children, but how many and would they be buried there also? Was I going to find out that she had died young in 1848, and the window was a commemoration from her husband or family?

The onion was being slowly unpeeled, but I felt I wasn't doing a very good job at my sleuthing.

# Chapter 14
## A Visit to the Cemetery

I knew where the cemetery was in Terrassée. I had been there before several times just to look at the unusual way that the French bury each other. Hidden behind a high wall, the cimetière was reached by, for me, the alarmingly named Rue de Paradis, Paradise Street. It makes you wonder if anyone ever stands beside a grave here and says to himself or herself, "If there is any justice in this world, she's in hell shoveling shit right this minute." Not all of us are so forgiving as the street name would suggest. And it is hardly a street. Just a short stretch of country road lined densely with short, heavily leafed trees. A street that becomes sadder with every step you take down it. The cemetery gates lie at the end, flanked by two stone benches for those who wish to compose themselves, either before or after a visit with their loved ones.

Inside, tall cone-shaped Italian pines here and there against the walls and large brilliant plastic flowers on the graves are the only suggestion of living things. There is no grass. Pale gravel surrounds the graves and paves the walkways through them. The graves protrude from the ground, often with disconcerting photographs of the interred set in some kind of porcelain frame decorating them. And a large bouquet of garish pink and yellow and purple plastic roses set firmly atop. Perhaps for country people real flowers, which fade and fall apart in a few days, are not enough of a remembrance. Or perhaps it saves them from having to visit very regularly.

There are mausoleums dotted here and there in the cemetery of Terrassée, several with large iron chains drooped about them, marking the size of the family plot. The Contant de Cazas family did not have this kind of memorial. Instead, they had a small stone monument echoing the Egyptian "Cleopatra's Needle" plinth that Napoleon erected in the center of the Place de Concorde in Paris. Two neat rows of stone tombs stood on either side of this monument. All of these tombs seemed older than the rest of the tombs in the cemetery. They were carved of a semiporous dark gray stone, and lichen has covered this stone in many places, as it had the four sides of the central plinth. Names and dates had once been carved on this, but they were almost impossible to discern. No one else was in the cemetery so I didn't hesitate to stand very close and scrape at the greenish gray lichen. I was able to make out COMTESSE DE CAZAS and the date of OCTOBER 1847 cut into the stone. Did this mean that my Countess, Catherine, had died an early death?

There were eighteen tombs in all, placed facing each other with the monument in the center of the two ranks. I went to the far end and began working my way down. The first tomb seemed to contain a number of people. There seemed to be a child that must have born stillborn as there was only a single date of 20 July 1838. His name was Charles Albert.

Interred with him seemed to have been a couple. Or perhaps not. Édouard had been born in 1840 and died in 1907. He seemed to have been born in September. That was all I could make out. Buried with him was a woman. Could it have been his wife? She could have been Catherine, and she died in 1871 at the age of sixty-two. It was added below her death date. "PRAY FOR HER."

That didn't make sense. Could Charles Albert have been a child of Catherine? And Édouard another son, born just a year later? Buried in his mother's grave with his stillborn brother? Perhaps. At least my very active imagination put it together in that way. We would have to see what else I could find out.

It was growing cold in the cemetery, and the eternal gray skies of France were closing in overhead. I made my way out of the cemetery past the protuberant graves, the glazed last photographs of those who lay beneath them . . . Amelie, who was quite pretty and must have died in the late 1950s from her dress and hairdo . . . Jean-Charles, an old, old man with still fiery eyes and a white mustache who must have fought in the First World War. There was a kind of military decoration attached to his tomb . . . Pierre, that ladylike face and those curls so carefully arranged. Could he have been a hairdresser? Did he try to get local girls to wear their hair like Sylvie Vartan in the 1970s? There they all were, resting quietly under their slabs of stone and garish plastic flowers. Some of the flowers were ceramic. They would truly last forever in their brilliant gaudiness. Bright purple pansies under the snow that was coming. I closed the large iron gate behind me and walked down the Rue de Paradis, now very somber under the branches that met overhead from the tightly packed trees. I went home and lit a large fire in the kitchen fireplace. The world seemed warm, or at least I did.

**Chapter 15**
**Fifth Letter from Le Rivage**


20 March 1838

My Dear Aunt,

Spring is coming to our flat, flat countryside. From the end of
the allée of trees that line the road to our front door one can look off
across the countryside, brown now for so many months, and there is
a faint haze of green across some of the fields. The sky still looks as
though it is suffering from cold, but it is blue. However, a very, very
pale blue. The first flowers begin to appear. The jonquils are
popping up through the grass on the lawns, and there is one big bush
in the courtyard covered in bright yellow blossoms. I do not know its
name. It is not a plant that we have in the south. I must ask my
husband its name.

My maid Minette has just married but that does not interfere
with her duties as she has married one of the men on the estate here.
There is a nice little cottage available among the outbuildings, which
was empty, and they are already living there. We had the ceremony
here in our salon, and I gave her one of my dresses as a wedding
gown. The pink one, which I realized I was never going to wear
here. We arranged a muslin insert in the top so she did not get
married with bare shoulders. She looked very pretty, and I know she
will be happy. Gilbert is a good-looking and well setup man. You
have an eye for good-looking men and you would approve.

Dressing gown in the fashion worn by Catherine.

Why have I forgotten to tell you that I visited Paris with my husband at the end of February? Curious that I would have not started my letter with such important news. There is still no train, but by coach with an overnight stop in Orléans it was rapidly done.

We arrived in Paris, and what a maelstrom! There seemed to be hundreds of small fiacres, small two-person carriages not at all like anything we have seen in the countryside. My husband, being large and strong, managed to get us and our bags through the crowd and into a carriage. I clung to him like a drowning person in a shipwreck. Our hotel was on the Quai des Grands-Augustins, and we were soon there.

Perhaps because I had given a dress to my maid, my husband was insisting that I have several new dresses made. We went the next day to a seamstress so that they could be finished while we were in Paris and I could take them back with me. I suppose I am to shine among our local ladies with my new Parisian dresses.

The style now in Paris is even larger sleeves than we have been used to, set low on the arm. The skirts no longer touch the ground, and this makes me a little uneasy. However, I bent my will to Dame Fashion and allowed the seamstress to make them the length she felt was fashionable. One can see my feet and some of my ankle quite clearly when I walk in these dresses. It makes me feel as though I am again a young girl when we paid little attention to the length of our skirts and ran and played with our dogs and climbed trees with abandon.

I have one dress in something of a plaid. Not really écossais scotch plaid but green on green in a woven pattern very much like the plaids we know. I will wear it to church for the most part, I would imagine. The seamstress has a coworker who makes hats and bonnets and created for me a really beautiful arrangement of eyelet lace in white on a comb with long streamers of the lace coming down from behind to rest on my shoulders. It is beautiful and very fragile, and I will insist on a box for it all by itself so that is will not be crushed.

I have another dress that is a kind of gentian blue in a solid color, simply made with a separate insert at the top, so that it can be worn with a more open neckline in warm weather. It, too, has the mandatory large sleeves, and there is also a kind of capelet or small cape that covers the shoulders and buttons up to the neck with the front flaps that fit under the rather wide belt. All made of the same material. I have a new bonnet to go with this as it can be worn for shopping and visiting very nicely with its capelet and will serve me well at Le Rivage. The weather can be very changeable around Terrassée and in this way, I can leave the house rapidly on errands without having to change my clothes completely. The bonnet has a small, round shape and has forget-me-nots fitting under the brim, rather than on top of the bonnet, which I find very pretty. Am I a fool to think that my eyes are one of my best features and having blue near them intensifies their color? And why should a married lady like myself even concern myself with these things? Perhaps our vanity is one of our most stubborn qualities to be erased.

—

Paris as it looked when visited by Catherine and Bernard.  The
Pont Neuf crossing the Seine River to the Louvre Palace.


But then again, why not? At least we have someone to truly love
. . . ourselves? I'm sure your eyebrows are almost touching the sky
as you read that last statement.

    While we were in Paris we had the great pleasure of visiting
the new Spanish wing of the Louvre. It was just opened in January
by the king. It has several wonderful paintings by Velázquez, I hope
I have spelled that right, of whom I had heard but never seen. You
feel that you are looking at a real person. His paintings are so very
lifelike, and yet, when you come close, you see that a pearl or the
gleam of an eye is just a little swipe of white paint! There is also the
famous El Greco, whose paintings are very beautiful but do not
make you feel that you are looking at real people. They make you
feel feverish and as though you are looking at things from
underwater. As though you are underwater. There are also paintings
by painters named Murillo and Zubaran. I do hope that I am spelling
these things correctly. There is a very deep atmosphere that
surrounds all those paintings that I suppose one must define. There
are heavy shadows and a kind of, could you call it "seriousness,"
about these paintings that contrast quite strongly with French
paintings. Our painters seem to paint something ideal and beautiful,
even when it is sad. The Spanish paintings look much more like real
people doing real things, but there is a strong feeling of sadness over
the subject. As though life was essentially a sad affair. I don't
believe this, nor do you. Am I right?

    We went to the theater one evening when my new green
dress was ready. It was on the Boulevard Italien, but I was
disappointed. The stage lights were very smoky, and our box seemed
to get the worst of it. The audience was very noisy and seemed to be
there as much to be seen themselves as to watch what was being
presented to them on the stage, which was largely some loud singing
and a lot of jokes, many of which I didn't understand. As I left,
many men I didn't know tipped their hats to me, which irritated my
husband a good bit, but, in fact, I think rather pleased him. He
muttered about it in the cab that took us back to our hotel but there
was certainly no communication that I had displeased him in any
way.

So to finish this letter that you must be getting very weary of reading . . . Paris is a very large and very noisy place that does not seem to ever really become quiet. There are always military troops trotting their horses through the streets, and carriages going this way and that. Many men are on horseback, and even, sometimes, they were accompanied by ladies. I imagine going to a park to take some exercise. Children run in front of and behind the horses, and there seems to be no semblance whatsoever of order or precedence.

I did have the great pleasure of seeing the Duke of Orléans pass with his equerries while we were out one day. He is a very dashing and tall man with fair hair and whiskers and a profile like a Greek statue. When you think that his father, the king, most closely resembles a pear, and his mother a white goat it is almost miraculous that he should be so handsome. One can understand how many hearts were broken when he married his little German princess last year. And there are no rumors about Paris that he is anything but a very attentive husband. The duchess of Orléans is awaiting her first child I am told, which will be born this summer.

I was very glad to have seen the heir to the throne, and I was equally glad to return to our calm harbor at Le Rivage. The life of a large city like Paris is not for me. There is an interesting series of articles beginning to be published in Le Rivage Française on religion. The first one is called the "The State of Souls." It caused me to think rather seriously about the state of my own. In many ways I feel that my life has proceeded rather calmly along its path and that, to my knowledge, I have never harmed another person in any serious way. I feel as though the same feeling I had as a child by your side I still have today. Does that make me childlike? Or innocent? And yet again, we may have sinned against others and had no idea that we have done so. But how are we then to know? We have never discussed these things before, and I wish very much to have your thinking. This is not something I can discuss with my husband. He would likely take me back to Paris and buy me more dresses. He is a very good man, but his fields hold the center of his interest.

I remain, as always, your very devoted niece who will hold you forever in my heart.

Catherine

# Chapter 16
## Sixth Letter from Le Rivage

21 April 1838

My Very, Very Dear Tante Mathilde,

This is my first spring at Le Rivage, and I am so enchanted by it I can hardly bear to remain in the house during the day. The sun has been shining brilliantly as though to call the flowers from their hiding within their buds. And they have come forth in a manner that is almost shocking.

Our spring in the south is much more gradual, and we are almost never without some flowers. Here they truly go away for long gray months, and when they come back, one feels one has almost forgotten how they looked. The fruit trees are miraculous, each one standing as though it were a bouquet, splashing an abundance of pink or white blossoms out of each small trunk. The cherry trees are my particular favorites, with their pink, pink, pink petals. When the wind blows, I run into the orchard so that I can stand in the blizzard of pink blossoms that fall about me. It is as though winter has become seduced by the power of the sun and has become warm, and each snowflake has become pink instead of white. It is only now that I regret giving my pink dress to my maid. I would have liked to be all in pink when the petals fly about and catch in my hair and stick to my face. The servants and my husband think I am a bit mad for finding their spring so lovely. They are used to it and are all caught up right now with making sure they have enough seed and beginning the first plowing for the spring wheat.

---

There are a few children here among the workers, and I encourage them to come with me for long walks along the hedgerows. The wildflowers are not long lived, and right now, all the fields and roadways are lined with tiny white flowers and the bright red coquelicot. They seem to be a brighter red here; perhaps it is the light.

The only thing to note other than this that you would like to hear about is my visit to the chateau of Chenonceaux, which is not very far from here. Perhaps an hour in a fast carriage. I received a note from the chatelaine, Mme. Dupin de Francueil, at the beginning of the month. She had seen me in Saint Marc it seems, inquired who I was, and was told the Countess Contant de Cazas (does that not sound strange to you as a title?) and wrote saying she would like to meet me and would it be possible for me to pay her a visit one day? My husband was very pleased with this invitation. He has never met M. and Mme. Dupin de Francueil but understands that they are very nice people. Mme. Dupin de Francueil is a cousin of the famous George Sand, who has visited there frequently in the past I was told. Although not noble, the family has married into noble families, and if I understand correctly, they are the most important family in our little piece of countryside.

I replied and suggested that a visit be made, perhaps for tea, on a Sunday ˘when my husband was not occupied with his estate and the work of the Chateau Le Rivage. I made a point of mentioning the chateau and signed my full name with a flourish, then sent it off by a servant to Chenonceaux.

The reply came the next day, and the following Sunday, we set off for Chenonceaux. My husband looked so handsome in his new blue coat and tall hat. I was pleased to be able to introduce him to the Dupin de Francueils. As for the Dupin de Francueils, they are a pleasant elderly couple whom I would guess are bored to death at Chenonceaux. Which goes to prove that one can be bored even in heaven, for that is what that chateau is like. One arrives passing through a long allée of very tall trees, lined with streams. My husband, who is a very well educated historian, explained to me that this is the very avenue that Mary Queen of Scots passed through to celebrate her marriage to Francis the Second, which made her the Queen of France. Did you know Mary Queen of Scots was the Queen of France before she was the Queen of Scotland? She was only Queen of France a few years. Her husband died young, and she then went to Scotland. The old queen was Catherine de Médicis whose ladies-in-waiting, called the Flying Squad, were dressed as mermaids and were posed along the banks of these streams beside the avenue playing musical instruments and singing in the torchlight that lit the wedding party. Doesn't that sound romantic and beautiful? I was also told that the Flying Squad was directed to have romantic liaisons with important men in the court so that the old queen could get reports on everything that was being planned and discussed behind her back. So different from our times, isn't it? I think it is very unlikely that Queen Marie-Amélie would delegate her ladies-in-waiting to behave similarly. Today, it would be a scandal!

The gardens of Chenonceaux are quite dreamlike. Drawing up in front of the chateau, you see them on either side. They were the work of Diane de Poitiers, who was the favorite of Henry the Second, who was married to Catherine de Médicis.

We know all of this from our history lessons, of course, but it is quite a different thing to actually tread the same paths among the multicolored flowers in the gardens created by the beautiful Diane to bewitch Henry II.

M. and Mme. Dupin de Francueil came out to greet us, and we were taken inside. Although the chateau is very beautiful in the Renaissance manner, it is not very large. They have it very well appointed and furnished as though it were simply a large country home. There were fires burning in the large fireplaces, and it was quite warm and "cozy" within. (The Countess wrote "cozy" in English.)

—

I was very glad that I had worn my new blue dress with the capelet, as it was warm enough in the chateau to remove the capelet so I could show something of my shoulders, which my husband thinks are among my best points. One can always enjoy being shown off a bit if it makes one's husband happy.

After tea, we strolled in the gardens, and there one can truly see the most amazing feature of the chateau. It is built completely across a river! It's true. It is quite astonishing. No one, in all their discussions of George Sand and Mary Queen of Scots and Diane de Poitiers, ever mentioned this phenomenon. Evidently, the chateau was originally a fortified mill, built a bit into the river so the river could run around it and create a kind of natural moat. When

Diane de Poitiers was given it, she built a bridge from the riverside of the chateau to the opposite bank of the Cher River. She did this to allow the king to cross the river for his hunting without having to ride up or downstream to find a bridge.

Catherine de Médicis took Chenonceaux away from Diane de Poitiers when the king was killed in a jousting match, and then built a ballroom on the bridge. The Dupin de Francueil have since then built an additional floor on the ballroom. To see this gigantic structure on its thick pillars with the river running directly under it is to blink one's eyes in disbelief. It is almost makes one believe the fairy stories, where one can climb a beanstalk into the sky.

I asked if I could re-enter the chateau to stand in a window and see the river running under my feet, and they were pleased to lead me back inside and down the large entry hall and into the ballroom. This large white room leads on and on and on, and midway down it, I stepped to a window and saw the river running swiftly below me. It was like flying and quite unlike simply standing on a bridge and letting water flow below you. Ensconced as I was in a large ballroom, seeing the water flow beneath my feet had a great feeling of magic. I think M. and Mme. Dupin de Franceuil were pleased that I enjoyed the experience, and my husband smiled on me benevolently as though I were four years old. We then departed as it was coming to the close of the afternoon. We were back at Le Rivage just as the day was ending. We left our hosts at the chateau with an invitation to come visit us, which I do not think they will do as I do not imagine they leave Chenonceaux very often, but I now feel that when I have guests I would not be unwelcome to take them to Chenonceaux to see the magnificent gardens.

On our return home, my husband told me that when Diane de Poitiers was dispossessed of Chenonceaux, she was given the chateau of Chaumont in exchange, where she lived a number of years before departing for her own family chateau in Normandy. I should like very much to visit Chaumont one day also. My husband added his own disquisition upon Diane de Poitiers that she bathed in cold water every day and was reported to have retained her beauty throughout her lifetime. She was much older than Henry the Second and had actually escorted him, with her husband, to the Spanish border when his brother and he were exchanged as prisoners of war for their father, Francis the First. He evidently was captured by the Spanish at the Battle of Milan.

Amazing that I remember all this, isn't it? What the French and Spanish were doing battling in Milan in Italy I didn't ask as I am certain I will never remember it.

For me, it was a lovely day and doubly lovely as I got to spend it entirely alone with my husband. Which, in itself, is a very rare opportunity.

Now, enough boring stories about chateaux. Adieu, my dear aunt. Write me soon with your news. I remain your devoted niece.

Catherine

# Chapter 17
## Seventh Letter from Le Rivage

29 May 1838

My Dear Aunt,

Now, my dear aunt, I have true news for you. I am going to have a child! I have waited until the very end of the month to be completely certain. I had a suspicion of it last month but wanted to be very certain. Now each morning I am very sick and very happy all the same time. My maid has discovered that she, too, is going to have a child, so we are going to be waiting for our little ones at almost exactly the same pace. This is comforting to me, if rather foolish!

It is comforting to me too, as now the work of the chateau is in full flourish and my dear husband is not very present. The planting is underway, and the courtyard is whirling with horses and wagons and men and women it seems almost the entire day and well into the evening. We are now approaching the longer days of the year. Even as late as ten o'clock in the evening, it is still broad daylight and one sits at the dinner table thinking that somehow it is still seven o'clock.

To think that next year at this time I will have my own little baby to carry about and to stand under the falling cherry petals—a boy or girl, I shall dress the baby in pink!

This is all I am going to write about today as I am too excited to remain at my desk. I must go out and walk down our long drive to the end where I can stand and see the great stretch of fields of Le Rivage reaching almost all the way to the outskirts of Terrassée. What a year lies before us! How good the world is.

With my deep and unending affection, your niece,

Catherine

# Chapter 18
## A Letter from Aunt Mathilde


Editor's note:

This letter from Mathilde, Comtesse de Cazas, was found among the letters to her from her niece Catherine. Undated, it seems to have been a first draft of a letter that she may have changed in some ways before sending it to her niece. At the top in her handwriting in a somewhat larger size has been written "Retunu." Retained for what reason we do not know, but she evidently thought it was important and placed it with the letters to her from her niece.

It is interesting to note that that her signature at the end "Mathilde de Cazas" indicates the level of formality maintained by an older woman toward a younger woman at this time and also that she was evidently not a blood relative but the wife of Catherine's uncle, the brother of her father. Despite its formality, the letter is unusual for it directness. It has been placed here as, although undated, it seems to be the first recognition of the young Countess's pregnancy.


My Dear Niece,

What rich and wonderful news that you are to become a mother. This will be a great blessing for you, as I know that you have an unusually strong feeling for children. And now you will be able to lavish that affection on your own. I embrace you very strongly, and my prayers will be with you constantly in your newfound happiness.

My thoughts have been with you a great deal since I received your letter, and I wish to let you into my brain with a complete openness as I feel many women share experiences but choose not to discuss them as perhaps being too intimate. There is no one in the world to whom I feel closer and so feel entitled to share these thoughts than with you.

I believe for a woman to feel that she has completed the path that destiny has set her feet upon she must fulfill for a man his great desire to leave children behind as a testimonial that he has passed across the face of the earth. We women have an entirely different relationship with the earth and heavens above. Each month we are reminded of the suffering of our Lord and how fragile our own lives are. And that, also, we are here for a purpose. Moody creatures that we are, we feel elated with the sun, depressed when we must live beneath gray skies. I often think that if the moon is powerful enough to move the waters of the sea up and down in powerful tides of movement in its passage through the skies, how must it affect us also, making the blood pull and surge from our brains and hearts. We are well aware of these phenomena. Men are not, and to them if there is no logical explanation for an event then it has not taken place.

It is quite clear from your letters that the Count is much taken up with his chateau and his estate. So much better this is than the exploits of his brother, who wishes only to marry below himself and live on the money his brother provides him. How much more fortunate you are in being married to the older brother rather than the younger.

I believe the Count does love you in his way, which is the way of holding our world together in the succession of families and the taking of responsibility for land. You are part of this knitting together of the fabric of life. You are a wife of whom, I am sure, he is proud. A wife for whom no excuses need to be made. Your lineage is pure, your intellect is excellent, and you have your share of beauty. All things that any man wishes to have passed on to the generations that follow.

And there are two other things that one need not skirt around. You are twenty-seven years of age. Because of our isolated position in the country and because you have had no mother from a tender age, your father was very remiss in not seeking suitors for your hand when you were much younger. But one did arrive at your door and found you pleasing. For this, you must count yourself among the lucky. And there is also the subject of your title which, unarguably, weighed in the balance in your husband's choice. This was certainly not his reason for marrying you, but it tipped the scales to some degree most certainly. You did not come with a sizeable dowry, so your title had to stand in its stead. I should add, your title would have meant nothing if you were not agreeable to him.

The fact that he has adopted your title for himself is of no moment. Your title is your title. It can never be taken away from you. That he has chosen to pass it on to your children may not be habitual historically speaking; it may even be unique. But that is how the situation stands and you must adapt to it. Truly, it is not very important. What is important is how your life pleases you as it passes day by day. Soon you will have a child, and I imagine you will have a number of them. Soon you will be completely occupied with them. Soon the fact that your husband does not have the lineaments of some dashing hussar who wishes to crush you in his arms at all times will become unimportant. I know of what I speak. I married your uncle because he was a fine man and our families had known each other for a long time. I never had a great passion for him and yet today I love him very much. In much the same way that I love our children, but even so it is a great love.

And perhaps I am not going too far when I bring up your unfortunate preoccupation with Balthazar Roche. Now de la Roche, I notice, which is quite amusing. I do not believe that his courting of you was ever very serious on his part, and I think he never clearly understood what an emotional and dedicated young miss you were. His sudden departure and pursuit of Caroline de Kerteguy when she arrived here from Martinique only underlines how his only serious pursuit was that of a fortune. An heiress to a sugar fortune appearing as if from heaven drew him like a fly to honey. My dear, my dear, my dear. I know only too well how broken your heart was, but believe me, it was the gods smiling upon you when he moved out of your life. And they have smiled upon you again by placing you in the very competent and responsible hands of your husband—who, may I remind you, is a tall and handsome man in his own right. Perhaps he is not a Don Juan. In my eyes that is only an advantage.

So there, my angel, all the cards have been placed on the table. I have unburdened all the thoughts from my brain and the emotions from my heart. You will not receive such a letter from me again. It is not given to us to know our destiny. Many times the things we wish for are not the things that are best

for us. We must turn ourselves over to the river of life and swim in the direction it carries us. Otherwise, we run the risk of exhausting ourselves and sinking. Well, there it is. I must stop before I make myself ridiculous.

With great and enduring affection, I remain,

Mathilde, Countess de Cazas

---

## Chapter 19
## Eighth Letter from Le Rivage

3 July 1838

My Dear Aunt,

What a brave letter you have written me. Many of the things you discuss I have already pondered in my heart. I wish to reassure you that I do not feel that I am in the wrong place doing things that I do not wish to do. There is a great need for me in the place I occupy here at Le Rivage. Just ensuring that everyone who has an occupation here at the chateau and on its lands is fed correctly, clothed appropriately, and has their illnesses and injuries properly taken care of, that alone makes me feel worthy. In the past, my husband has taken care of these things, and I believe that he always took care of them well, but he is not a woman, and I think a woman's care is more appreciated by those receiving the attention from their chatelaine.

I think, also, the fact that I am not a young girl gives them more confidence that their mistress has some knowledge of what she is doing, whether that is true or not.

And curiously, and this is a subject that we will not discuss again, the fact that I am a Countess gives pride to all those who are associated with the chateau. I hear them say "La Comtesse wishes . . ." or "It is for La Comtesse and . . ." It is quite clear that they enjoy this and feel more important because of it. If my title can serve to give them pride in themselves and their work, so be it. I could not ask more.

And now to baby. I am certainly filling out and am larger around in the waist than I have ever been. I believe that my child's life began during our visit to Paris, but perhaps I am wrong. We shall soon see. For the moment, I am still riding every day so as to have some healthy exercise. The doctor here tells me that this is not risky in the first months. I plan to stop at the end of the month. The weather here is so beautiful now, and one is always so aware of the gray world that awaits us after the harvest is in.

You would be much amused to see me very involved with my knitting. You know how I have always abhorred handiwork as the occupation of not only the small-minded but also the completely empty-headed. The very idea of embroidery or sewing dainty little things always seemed to be such a waste of time. But here I am, having emptied my head, with a needle in each hand, knitting very happily. My maid Minette is very expert at these kinds of activities, and since she is expecting a little one also, we can spend hours and hours together preparing for the events ahead, knitting little jackets and hats. I have made a quite pretty blanket already, which I bound in pink satin ribbon. Not for the baby's bed, but more for carrying the baby about with me. I don't plan to be separated from my child for a minute. I am undoubtedly going to be one of those horrendous mothers who want to keep their child with them their whole lifelong.

I also had the seamstress here to begin making me some fuller gowns to wear. I do not plan to appear much in public, but should that eventuality arise, I have a kind of eighteenth-century garment being made in lavender with little sprigs of flowers on it. Something like a Watteau painting. The color suits me very well, actually, though I have never worn it before. I wonder why not. Too pretty, most probably.

In the newspaper last month, I read that Lamartine had published a new work so I wrote away for it. It is called La Chute d'un Ange (The Fall of an Angel). It is very moving and very romantic. Of course, the kind of thing that you most probably feel I should not be reading as it only encourages that stubborn Romantic element in character. However, I want my child to be sensitive, whether it be a boy or girl, so I am trying to expose myself to beautiful sights and beautiful thoughts and beautiful feelings as much as I can in this period, which I am actually enjoying very much.

And now, dear Aunt, I leave you. Your letter was very instructive, and I am not so hopeless as you suppose as I had already considered a good many of the subjects you discussed in it.

With a full heart and what is becoming a very full body, I shall always remain your constantly loving niece,

Catherine

# Chapter 20
## Ninth Letter from Le Rivage


25 July 1838

My Dear Aunt Mathilde de Cazas, I hope that you will not feel that I am being unduly familiar by addressing you in this familiar a manner. It is with the greatest regret that I am writing you to tell you that Catherine has suffered a fall from her horse and our child has been lost to us.

It has caused great unhappiness to both Catherine and myself. And she has asked that I write to you as she has insufficient force of emotion at this time to write to you herself.

I feel myself very much to blame for this situation as Catherine has been ill at ease in riding by herself on her new horse, and I have urged her to conquer her fears. She was riding alone, returning to Le Rivage, when her horse made an attempt to run away with her, and when she reined the horse in, it threw her. Not so very forcibly, as you know that she is an accomplished horsewoman, but she fell. She remounted the horse thinking that she not injured herself, but by the time she arrived at Le Rivage it was quite evident that an injury had been done. I sent immediately for her doctor in Terrassée, but it was impossible to save our child. It would have been a little boy. We have christened the infant and interred him in the Terrassée cemetery with his ancestors. It is all very sad.

Bernard Contant as a young man. Before becoming Comte Contant de Cazas.


Catherine's health has been my greatest concern, and she seems to not have harmed herself in any serious way. Please send your prayers to us at this very unfortunate time.
  With all of my very warmest feelings,
Your nephew, Bernard

**Chapter 21**
**Editor's Note**


After her riding accident and the loss of her child, Catherine, Countess Contant de Cazas, does not correspond with her aunt Mathilde for a number of months. I think it is entirely possible that her aunt came to the Cha teau Le Rivage to be with her at this difficult time, or perhaps Catherine was not able emotionally to bring herself to correspond.

I believe that it may very well be the former as there are no letters in her aunt's collection from Le Rivage at all during this time period.

Her letters begin again shortly before Christmas of 1838, so we know that her aunt is definitely in her own home in the south by this time.

## Chapter 22
## The Tea Party


From D. D. Abercrombie's Journal:

I wonder if other people ever feel the pull of destiny thickening around them. It is something like déjà vu. I always feel when I have the experience of repeating an episode from a dream that it indicates being on the right track of your life. The track is there if only we can find it. I think that those people who are unhappy with their lives are those who somehow have slipped off their track. Lured by a monied marriage or fame-giving job or simply holding back out of fear they have gotten off their own destiny's path.

And when you are on your destiny's path, do the clues fall more heavily into place all the time? They seem to. Only this afternoon as I was coming home, the Comtesse got out of her car directly in front of my door. Simultaneously, Mademoiselle Cartelage was sortieing forth from the gates of the abbey where she serves as a guide, as I've noted before. Mademoiselle's father was the local photographer and recorded the village's life for many years. His collection is in the abbey as a small kind of photo museum.

The two women embraced gingerly. They evidently had gone to school together here in the village at some point, which surprised me. I hadn't imagined the Comtesse going to school here but, of course, she must have done so during the war. She never mentioned it, nor had Mademoiselle Cartelage in her first visit to my home.

Mademoiselle is a very forthright woman, something of a village character, blocky in build, hairy of the upper lip. Never married and perhaps an undeveloped lesbian. Her parents' former home, which is tiny, is around the corner from me and lived in by her diminutive brother and his wife. Large Irene has an equally large house out on the edge of town. Like so many daughters, she is probably like her dark and forceful father. Her brother is like his invisible self-effacing mother.

Mademoiselle Cartelage said, "Can we come in? We used to attend church school in this building. Remember, Nathalie? Your grandmother taught us how to dance here. Remember? Wasn't it you who got up on the kitchen table and danced? I remember it well."

Irene swept the Comtesse and I into the house, which I was not unwilling to do if these were the kind of confidences I was about to hear. In my kitchen she looked about and said, "Yes, this is the room in which we were taught dancing." She looked as if she was about to seize the Comtesse and waltz about the room. The Comtesse moved to safety on the other side of the table.

We went into the garden. I asked if they would have time to take tea with me. They did. As they seated themselves at the garden table Irene looked down the garden walk and said, as she had during her first visit, "That's where the privy stood. Out there. It was cold in there."

When I brought the tea and some cookies that I luckily had bought that morning to the table, Irene was saying, "But your family owned this house, Nathalie, didn't they?"

I asked, "But what was it used for? Wasn't it an inn?" Irene said, "I think it was a kind of rooming house where people who worked at the abbey stayed. And perhaps some students. The building down past the church was an extra dormitory. I know that. The abbey was a very important school, you know. I've heard that at one time, of course long ago, that Oxford, Cambridge, and our abbey were the three most important schools in Europe."

I said, "But surely there were important schools in Paris?"

Irene replied, "Perhaps," in that French manner that suggests that you are entirely wrong and know nothing, but that the speaker is being polite.

The Comtesse added, "The abbey always had boys of all ages, so I think it was quite different from Oxford and Cambridge. And it wasn't really a college, at least in my family's time. One left the abbey school at about the age of eighteen, I believe."

Irene was not to be deterred. "But your family owned this house, I'm sure of it. It was empty except for those Saturdays when we girls used to come here, or perhaps there were people living upstairs. We came to learn how to sew and cook and those things we needed to know for later when we were married." She laughed heartily. "I never had to use any of them." And laughed very jollily again as though nothing could have pleased her more.

"I remember your grandmother so well. Always in black. But pretty black. She was a pretty woman, your grandmother," she said to the Comtesse. "And she was always afraid to go upstairs. Do you remember that?"

The Comtesse did not really respond. Her social training probably was that it was not only bad manners to talk of yourself but also of your family . . . particularly when it was superior to anyone else's around you.

"I remember when your family came to church. I was very small, of course. It was before the war. But they still came in from the cha̍teau in a carriage and four. There were plenty of cars about, but your family still came into the village in their carriage."

The Comtesse said weakly, "I'm sure we had a car."

Irene went on, "You were probably too small to be taken to church. I don't remember you being in the carriage. Only later, when we were all here together."

"When did your family sell the house?" I asked the Comtesse. I realized immediately that this was a vulgar question and one a really nice person would never ask as it involved money and real estate.

"I think the family you bought it from purchased it from my brother," the Comtesse offered in a low tone. Almost an aside, as though she was telling me something quite personal and only was doing it as we were good friends, "But they were not in it very long. They divorced before renovating it," she added.

As they got up to leave she said, as though she was just remembering it and could have easily forgotten it, "I have some more letters from my ancestor to her aunt. I mentioned your interest to my cousin Beatrice, who lives in Toulouse, and she had some things among her effects. I told her that you were extremely careful with those that I loaned you, so she has sent me the packet she had. There are not many, but they are, I think, more interesting. Evidently my ancestor, the Comte, had a rapprochement with a brother from whom he was estranged. I never knew that. And the Comtesse had her child at that time too. My great-grandfather."

"Was he blond?" I asked. I don't know why.

"You do ask curious questions!" the Comtesse said. "Yes, he was. I was blonde as a child too. They always said it came down from my great-grandfather and the old Comtesse's side of the family."

"You had beautiful hair. Long curls," Irene said to the Comtesse.

The Comtesse laughed. "I'm still blonde, but I'm afraid it's no longer due to my great-grandfather." The two women marched off down the village street side by side, the Comtesse to do her shopping, Irene to go home. I had arranged that I would drop by the cha teau the next day to pick up the letters.

# Chapter 23
## Another Letter from
## Catherine to Her Aunt

From D. D. Abercrombie's Journal:

The French are very curious. Speaking with them is like picking up broken glass with your bare hands. You must keep your eyes wide open and stay alert. When I called the Comtesse the following day I didn't call too early or too late. Too early would indicate that I was very anxious to read the new letters from Catherine to her aunt. If I called too late it would indicate that I wasn't interested enough. Most French people are always on guard in the hope that they will be offended.

An aside. People seem to complain to the degree that they feel they do not control their lives. Does the fact that the French are in an almost constant state of complaint indicate that the entire country does not feel in control of its own destiny? Entirely possible.

At any rate, I called the Comtesse at eleven. She could not feel that she had been awakened. If she had, it was not to her credit. And she could not yet be swept off in the duties of her day. She was there. No, it wasn't too early. No, she did not want to go to lunch as she did not want to leave the house while the maid was there. (Maid of some twenty or thirty years, probably, who might still steal a silver spoon or two.) I could come out any time to see the letters.

"Before lunch?" I asked.

"Certainly." But there was no offer of lunch at her home.

By eleven thirty I was there, pulling up in front of her large farmhouse in my ancient Peugeot. She was at the door. In her sitting room we examined the letters. The Comtesse did not offer me a cup of tea or coffee. The French don't do that sort of thing.

The letters were familiar looking. Again, the small envelope, the thick paper, the package of only three letters tied with a length of pale blue ribbon, probably not as old as the letters.

"My cousin had these tucked away in her writing desk," the Comtesse said. "She said they had always been there, so the desk very likely had belonged to that ancient old lady, the sister of the famous Catherine's father. I remember seeing that desk when I was in Toulouse. It must have been inherited even then, as it's certainly from the eighteenth century. It's a pretty desk." There was a faint note of envy in the Comtesse's voice.

She handed me the small packet. "I haven't read them. But I know you're fascinated with the past, so please take and copy them out if you wish. You can tell me what they say."

It suddenly dawned on me that with the Comtesse's sketchy education during the war perhaps she did not read with great ease. I don't think anyone was particularly interested in the education of an upper-class girl at that time. A boy, yes.

My heart was beating faster as I pulled out of her driveway, the packet of letters on the worn gray upholstery of the seat beside me. Why was I so fascinated by this slow picking apart of an old story, this slow tugging at loose ends, like trying to sort out a tangled skein of wool?

When I sat at my own old flat desk I stared at the little packet before me. I knew that in these letters I could find out whether the unsigned letters I had been reading were from the Comtesse Catherine or not. I quickly saw that they were. They had to be.

My Very Dear Aunt,
It has been quite a long time since I have written. My spirits were low after the loss of my child, and I felt it better not to burden others with my own sadness. Everyone has their own personal sadnesses. There is no reason for them to be made heavier with the misfortunes of their friends and family.

But recently, time is healing that wound and new friends have entered my life and some very interesting family complications are giving new interest. Quite by chance, I have met a young man here who has a connection to my brother-in-law. The brother-in-law and his family whom I have never met.

This young man, Gilles de Thorigny, is a military officer on leave of absence who is teaching at the abbey here in the village. He is of excellent family, and his cousin is already a well-regarded officer in the army of some rank. Which all bodes very well for the young Monsieur de Thorigny.

As a single young man he has made the acquaintance of many families with eligible daughters here in the region, and through these contacts, his acquaintances are many. When we met he immediately asked me if I was a relative of the Contant family in St. Marc. I told him I believed I was, but that as I had married into the family not too long ago, I had never had the pleasure of meeting them.

He was quite amusing. He said, "But St. Marc is only five leagues away."

I said, "In some families a league can be longer than it is in other families." And we both laughed.

He is very agreeable, and it was good to laugh with him. I should mention also that he is a very handsome blond young man, so you can well understand why the hearts of the young women in our neighborhood are all aflutter.

I know what you are thinking, but please do not do so. I must be at least five years older than Monsieur de Thorigny and a very settled married lady. But I'm sure you know how contact with lighthearted youth can be so beneficial when one is emerging from the shadows of grief.

More important and more interestingly, through this young man I have met my brother-in-law and his wife and their children. I have not told my husband that I have made this rather daring connection because of the falling out between his younger brother and himself some time ago. I believe it was because my husband felt the bride was unworthy of admittance to our family. There were inheritance reasons also. At any rate, I feel sure you are longing to hear about the encounter.

You must be also be cluck-clucking at the idea of a wife deceiving her husband in this way, but to be entirely truthful, I see very little of him these days. He is very occupied with the chateau and its farms and grounds. He arises before I do and is gone to the fields before I breakfast and rarely returns for the midday meal. Because of the demands of the day he is early to bed, and our only time together is dinner. That time is largely spent in discussing his day, so you can easily see that any absences on my part would scarcely be noticed.

So one day recently I announced that my maid and I would go to St. Marc to buy material for new sheets and pillowcases, which is always a necessity and which we truly were planning to do. To our little itinerary we also added a brief stop to take tea with my relatives in the company of Monsieur de Thorigny whom, it seems, is very friendly with them. I find this reassuring as Monsieur de Thorigny is of impeccable family background and is not going to count among his friends those who are not worthy of him.

My brother-in-law and his family live in a neat, if admittedly small, house as one descends the hill into St. Marc. St. Marc is an ancient town, and the castle looms on the hill over the road. The small stone house is pleasantly situated on this road at the edge of the village, and its situation, I'm sure, makes it easy for the lady of the house to do her shopping and see that her children are dispatched to school.

The house abuts on the street with a garden behind with a few small outbuildings. They apparently keep a few chickens for eggs.

Madame is a fair-complexioned, light-haired lady somewhat shorter than myself who has kept her figure. She was nicely dressed in a dark-green bombazine without an undue number of petticoats with a fresh white collar, and there is really nothing to say that would be negative, either about her appearance or her manners.

Her husband, in a light blue coat and nankeen britches, is very much the gentleman. He does not closely resemble my husband as he has fairer hair and his blue eyes are more closely set together. He has, however, a nice appearance of intellectuality, and I was happy to see that there were a great many books in his home. This is always a good environment for children. I'm sure you will agree. Present also was a very small baby, not yet a year, I would guess. A little girl named Gabrielle. She was making attempts at walking and was altogether fetching. She should be a very pretty little girl. Her brother, a little boy named Thomas, was at that active two-year-old passage of life, but his mother kept him well occupied with little games. There are, it seems, three other children who were not at home. Five children seems quite a large family for a couple who have not been married such a very long time and whose home is not very large. And I probably should add, whose income is unknown, but the couple do not seem overly concerned, nor is there any appearance of poverty. So I do think that it behooves me not to be worried for them.

We did not at any point discuss the estrangement of the brothers, although they made it very clear that we were all members of the same family and that they were indeed pleased to meet me. They expressed their condolences at the premature loss of my child and sent their greeting to my husband. It is all mysterious in a very well-mannered way. At some point I will tell my husband that I have made their acquaintance, perhaps suggesting that it was more by chance than, in fact, it was and we will see what his reaction may be. If he wishes to have some rapprochement, this will give him the opportunity to do so. If not, we can then discuss it. I'm hoping that you will not perceive me as a disobedient wife but that in this modern world a woman can pursue, to some degree, a life of her own.

I should add that in our conversations I have discovered that my sister-in-law is the daughter of a most successful green grocer in St. Marc and is his only child, her mother having died at the time of her birth. She is certainly not someone who grew up as a scullery maid, scrubbing pots and pans in the kitchen of the local inn, even though employed as a maid at Le Rivage, and it is perhaps the largesse of her parent that makes the family's living situation as comfortable as it is.

—

On the ride back across the fields to Terrassée we had the company of Monsieur de Thorigny, who rode beside our carriage which we were able to keep open as the weather is extremely clement right now as the roadsides are bursting with scarlet poppies. Monsieur de Thorigny wanted to dismount and pick some for us, but I explained to him that they fade immediately once plucked, no matter how quickly they are placed in water. He is a very amusing man and, as I said, extremely handsome also. It is good to have such a lively new friend. I will have to introduce him to my husband very soon. I think he would have a good influence and perhaps interest him in something beside the affairs of the estate.

One last word, the wildflowers flow across the countryside in ever-changing patterns of color. Now it is the scarlet of poppies, then we have the lavender of lupine, and that followed by the white of Queen Anne's lace, and later blues, and then yellows. Through these beautiful months, fresh colors are forever arriving to meet our eyes.

I leave you with the fondest of thoughts, my much-beloved aunt,

> Your affectionate ---
> Catherine

**Chapter 24**
**Gilles de Thorigny**

From D. D. Abercrombie's Journal:

Why do I think the man in the basement is Gilles de Thorigny? Or was. Why do I even think it was a man? Because the Comtesse mentions him by name in her letters to her aunt? You know how it is when you are in love and no one knows about it. You want to hear your lover's name. You want to write your lover's name. You wonder if, in fact, your love has any basis in reality. And by mentioning that person's name you feel confirmed in your lover's existence.

Once I find that the Comtesse mentions him, and sometimes several times, in a letter, I begin to feel that I have to mention his name too. To make my suspicions real, I did this at another one of the Panaguas' parties. They are the most inveterate party givers anywhere around Terrassée, I guess because he was in the American consular service and must have gone to parties around the clock when he was working. He met Inez where? Madrid? Montevideo? At any rate, she loves parties just as much as he does. Or perhaps it keeps the both of them busy.

—

At their "cocktail" I saw again their neighbor, Colonel Lablancherie. The colonel is not at all the dashing ladies' man you might expect an ex-army man to be. He reminds me of Tweedledum or Tweedledee. He has a kind of firm body in the shape of a turnip with a firm little balding head fixed on top of it. He speaks in a slow, clear manner without emphasis and says really shocking things. He told me once at a party about serving in Indo-China with troops from Africa. While walking through the jungle with prisoners, one of his black sergeants took his machete and split the head of the prisoner who walking in front of him in two. The colonel was very clear about this: "Not sideways," he said, "but from top to bottom." Then the sergeant turned to the colonel and said, "He was annoying me." The colonel told this story because he knew his listeners would find it shocking and to demonstrate that he did not find it shocking himself. I often wondered what the colonel's private life included. Perhaps he fancied brutality in bed too. He concluded his story by saying of his experience in Indo-China, "It was a curious war but not unamusing."

Upon meeting him again I called him Colonel Lablancherie, and he said, "Please, call me Gilles." There are so many things that could mean in France. It could mean he fancied me. I somehow doubt that. He could be homosexual and is covering by being intimate. Or it could mean that he thinks he believes we are about the same age. He's probably right, but I'd hate to think so. It could mean that he likes me and is letting me past the eternal French barrier of "politesse." Somehow I doubt that too. Having no idea what his intentions were by such a statement I seized upon the name Gilles. Perhaps he could help me trace Gilles de Thorigny. Using neither colonel nor Gilles, I said, "What if one wanted to find out about someone who had once served in the French army? Is there some way to inquire about such a person?"

The colonel said, "When did they serve?"

I answered, "About 1840."

"1840? As early as that? Is this some relative of yours, Madame Abercrombie?" This was another of those French things. He had immediately noticed that I wasn't saying Gilles and knew I wasn't going to, so he called me by my most formal name. He used "Madame" instead of "Mademoiselle," which indicates that he does not consider me young, but of stature. A compliment and a disappointment all in one.

"No, no, not at all. I ran across something that makes me think a certain army officer lived in my house in the early part of the nineteenth century, and I thought I would try to find out about him," I said.

"How did you find out about him?" he inquired.

"I found his name and a date and a kind of insignia cut into the stone beside one of the bedroom windows. The stone carves so easily here, you know," I replied. I hoped that my complete lie sounded convincing.

"Bourré stone," he said.

"What was his name?" "Gilles de Thorigny."

"De Thorigny. De Thorigny. That's not a name from around here. Well, of course, you can contact the archives of the army. They keep very complete records, and you're lucky that it's not before the revolution as all of those files were destroyed. I'll get the address and you can write them a note. I'm sure they'll answer very promptly. They have nothing to do."

"Do you have my phone number?" I asked. "I could give you my card."

"Of course I have it," he said, not looking at me and headed off toward Inez Panagua and the drinks table.

The colonel did call me promptly the next morning with an address. The information source was at the French military museum in Paris, part of Les Invalides, the military hospital founded by Louis the Fourteenth. And the colonel was right about their promptness. I wrote, and a week later they replied. They said they had only two de Thorignys from that time period. Gustave—my heart sank, and Gilles—my heart leaped. The letter continued that they had very little information on Gilles de Thorigny but Gustave de Thorigny had risen to the rank of general and had retired only shortly before the end of the Second Empire. They were able to tell me that the de Thorignys seemed to have been cousins as the records indicated that their fathers were brothers and had also been in the army, and that their grandfather had been in the army also, but his records had been destroyed. They added that their records indicated the papers of Gustave de Thorigny had been deposited with the Musée de l'Armée. They would copy their files for two francs per page, and there were thirty-two pages in all for the two de Thorignys. If I would send a check or money order they would send me the document copies. I, of course, did this promptly but decided to contact the Musée de l'Armée while I was waiting.

Actually, I called the Musée and spoke with their librarian, who told me it would be necessary for me to come there to see their files as they did not make copies nor did they allow the materials in their library to be taken out. If I wished to make a copy of something that I found there that would be possible on the premises. For two francs a page. I wanted to tell her that it was only one franc a page at the post office but quickly realized that would unleash a torrent of French hostility in my direction that I could easily live without. So I went to Paris.

I was glad I did. They had boxes of things from Gustave de Thorigny that they had very evidently never gone through. A very nice man brought me box after box in a private reading room. I furrowed through them. I was not at all interested in Gustave but was hoping to stumble upon something about Gilles. In the fifth box I found them. It was so hard to believe that what I only fantasized about, in fact, existed. There in a bottom corner tied with what looked like a shoelace in leather were about twenty letters from Gilles de Thorigny to his cousin Gustave. I was told that it was now too late to copy them and that I would have to do it the following day. I did offer up, gently, the fact that I lived in the country and was told that the librarian would keep the packet of letters carefully at her desk so that I could start copying them as early as I wanted to the following morning. The library opened at nine. The librarian told me she would be on time in the self-satisfied manner the French have when they are able to deny you a service. Particularly when they are going to lose money by doing it.

There was nothing to it. I went to the inexpensive little Hotel des Croisés in the ninth arrondissement near La Trinité Church and threw myself on their mercy. They almost always have rooms, and they did that night. I ate at the café on the corner.

The next morning, wearing dirty underclothes, I was at the Musée promptly at nine o'clock and was handed over the bundle of letter by Gilles de Thorigny to his cousin Gustave. There were five in all. I retreated to the little reading room and saw immediately that after the first two or three letters he was mentioning the Comtesse de Cazas. Gilles's hand-writing was more difficult to read than the Comtesse's had been. He had probably been educated in military schools.

I immediately took them all to the librarian and was led to the copying machine. It wasn't easy, but they had been folded in larger size than the Comtesse's and were a little less fragile. It took several hours to copy all of them, and it cost eighty-eight francs finally, but I was able to catch the noon train out of the Gare d'Austerlitz. On the train I was able to start reading my copied letters. I was going to have to translate them, as well as the Countess's collection, to share this story with American friends. It was going to be very interesting seeing if the dates matched up. They were, of course, to his cousin. But even so, would the dates correlate with the Countess's letters to her aunt?

—

**Chapter 25**
**First Letter from Gilles**
**De Thorigny**


(Letter from Gilles de Thorigny to his cousin Gustave de
Thorigny, 4 September 1838)


My Dear Cousin,

How much you must have wondered where I have been and
what I have done since I parted from you in Grenoble in May. Now
that all the officers of my cavalry division have been given a leave of
absence for an unlimited time I have taken the opportunity to pursue
the charming Madame de la Tremoille, whom you may well
remember spent the winter with her husband on official business in
Grenoble. I was never sure whether my advances were being
considered or if she was only being her charming self to avoid any
possible political imbroglios for her husband's sake. Since she had
returned to Paris in the spring and I was free as a bird I decided to
visit one of my fellow officers there, le Comte Philippe de Rosier.
Do you remember him? A weedy and unimposing fellow but with
connections to the best families. Staying with him I was sure that I
would encounter the charming Ghislaine at one soirée or another.

I will not burden you with the details, but we did meet at
Philippe's aunt's home, and she suggested that I call upon her at one
of her little salons. I have a great penchant for brunettes and
particularly those with moles. It always suggests to me that there is a
warm nature under all those layers of lace and puffy sleeves.


———

I was fortunate that her husband was away on one of those . . . "boring" was the word Ghislaine used, official trips, and she seemed to welcome my suggestion that I drop in on her unexpectedly some day. Which I did, and the welcome was every bit as warm as I expected. Do you think that it is the advance of spring that makes women so welcoming? As with the other animals, to which our own race is certainly not unconnected, there seems to be an urge to breed in this season. Not that there isn't an urge to breed in all seasons, but more so at this time of year.

She was never willing that I spend the night, but we had merry romps on the chaise lounge of her boudoir. For myself, I prefer lovemaking when both parties are completely divested of their clothing, but this was never to be with Ghislaine. It was always skirts "up," breeches "down." Since I am a very modern man, this does not always please me as it requires a certain repetitiveness of position. It is very hard for a lady to be seated upon her recumbent male partner with the restriction of clothing, and I do not ever favor the standing position. I seem to be never able to keep my mind on what I'm doing when I am in a position to immediately leave the room.

However, this idyll was not to last for long as Monsieur de la Tremoille soon returned from Lyon or wherever he was, and I think the servants must have talked as my pretty lady was whisked away to her husband's estate and in my one interview with that gentleman, he made it abundantly clear that I would never be welcome there. Not in any way that could provoke a duel, but only in that extremely polite way, accompanied by smiles, that is a clear indication that one is not welcome and can never be considered a friend.

This situation, coupled with my need for money, my leave of absence pay having been run through rather quickly, has caused me to now find occupation at the cavalry school in an out-of-the-way place called Terrassée. Through my dear old aunt Christine, who is thicker than thieves with all the upper hierarchies of the church, I was put in contact with the bishop of Blois. For some reason not clear to me, the bishopric has some supervisory relation with the school in Terrassée, and upon inquiry, it was to be discovered that the school was sorely in need of a riding instructor, and furthermore, an instructor well versed in the use of arms on horseback. Which is surely true of myself.

---

And so, here I am, for how long I have no way of knowing, but not displeased. Terrassée is a rather ordinary small town, very typical of this region, but because the school is a famous and old one, there is an unusual number of aristocratic families here.

You will remember that when we were both pursuing our studies in Vendome that to be visited by our families was rare. With only Sunday afternoon as a time free of supervision and a few extra religious holidays our years revolved round upon round with little interruption. I believe that I often did not see my sisters for two or three years at a time. My father came to see the school officials occasionally and managed to squeeze in one other visit annually during which he was usually accompanied by my mother. But other than that, we saw very little of our loved ones. To remedy this similar situation here, many families have installed themselves in Terrassée, where their sons can visit them every Sunday after services. Their sisters are installed in a convent school not far from the abbey school so there are many fresh young faces to be seen in the narrow, winding streets of Terrassée.

The school was installed in what was an ancient abbey before the revolution, and there has been a school on these premises for many centuries. Eight to be exact. A knight of this region was aboard a foundering vessel in a storm on the Mediterranean Sea as he was returning from the Holy Land. This was well before the Crusades began. Surely he had been atoning for his sins by visiting Jerusalem, which had not yet fallen into the hands of the Muslims. The year was 1035. I know all of this from my landlord, who is deeply immersed in the history of his village, which is in fact not uninteresting. This knight was reported to be of great beauty. So beautiful he was called Gelduin the Girl. I have never heard this kind of attribution before, have you? It leads one to wonder what exactly were the sins of this Gelduin which had led him to visit Jerusalem.

To be brief, Gelduin prayed to the Virgin and swore that if he and the vessel were saved that he would found an abbey in this village. The Virgin fortuitously appeared in a cloud of snow over the ship, the seas immediately abated, and all aboard were saved. Gelduin, greatly relieved I would imagine, returned and did his duty, founding the abbey which had as its purpose the teaching of boys. Which, I would also imagine, was with the intention of creating more monks. And there you have it.

—

I have been fortunate to find a place to live in a large house that faces the gates of the school with a view of the chapel, which is called Our Lady of the Snows, in reference to the Virgin who appeared to Gelduin and was instrumental in the founding of the school. This chapel has never been finished, but even so, it is large and fronted with a beautiful rose window, which is certainly the equal of anything at the cathedral of Chartres. This has been a very rich abbey for centuries and always a school. That is clear from the size of the buildings and the remnants of the enormous walls that once circled the establishment. Undoubtedly, there were many people engaged in the care and feeding of those students entrusted to it. Monsieur Bourdin, my landlord, informs me that in the Middle Ages, the most important schools in Europe were Oxford and Cambridge in England and the abbey of Terrassée in our own country. This is a small town with a large history and its citizens bring up its history rather frequently.

When I first arrived in Terrassée, I put up at the Hotel de l'Ecole, a nicely kept small inn where relatives and friends stay when they come visit students. I rode my horse Etoile from Paris, taking the coach road, and made a three-day trip of it. I did not wish to ride Etoile hard, and there was no reason to, as the school did not expect me until the first of September. At the inn, when I inquired about a permanent residence, I was sent to Monsieur Bourdin, a local artisan who has saved his money and bought houses. He is now proprietor of a dwelling that has been many things, I would guess, in its long life. Three old houses joined together, it is a labyrinth of staircases, hallways, and rooms set at odd angles and different levels. Monsieur Bourdin informs me that it was originally three private dwellings that were combined and served as an inn for many years. Several hundred, I would think. Fortunately for me, there is a small stable in the courtyard, and I am able to keep Etoile in the same building with myself. I do not fancy keeping her with the other horses of the cavalry school. Horses learn bad habits from each other, and she is a mare with almost no bad habits. She does not bite her bit or press me against the side of the stable. And she is remarkably sure-footed. I think that often that is the case with horses with a star on their forehead. She is named for that star, and I often feel that she shares her good luck with me.

—

So what more can I tell you? I am well installed in a small and tidy room with a pleasant view of the Charles the Seventh Tower of the abbey as well as the gates and façade of the chapel. I have seen several pretty, or near pretty, maids moving about this house. I begin my classes with my students tomorrow. We shall see how well they ride. So far, I have no reason to regret my coming here. We shall see what destiny brings to here in Terrassée.

You have, as always, my most distinguished sentiments, my dear cousin,

Gilles de Thorigny

# Chapter 26
## Second Letter
## from Gilles de Thorigny


20 October 1838

My Dear Cousin Gustave,

I am beginning to settle in well in this little village of Terrassée. My room is very comfortable in the curious old house in which I have found living space. From my window I see the ancient Charles the Seventh tower that is one of the earliest parts of this old abbey, now a school. I also see the entrance gate and beyond that the chapel, only partially built, but its flying buttresses still make a wonderful sight with the birds flying in and out of them as the sun sets.

You will think me wildly imaginative when I tell you that I think the skies are quite a different color here than they are elsewhere in France. They are of a particularly clear blue that I have only seen before in some of the paintings in the important buildings in Venice. Could I call it Tiepolo blue? Next you will expect me to declare that I plan to become a painter. Little chance of that.

My students are young men of good family and have already had a certain amount of training in mounting a horse and staying there. Some of them have a very good seat and are allowed on Saturdays to leave the school and ride with the local hunt. A good many have their own horses that they have brought from their homes so the quality of horseflesh is good, for the most part. Also, the school has not been stinting on their purchases of horses for the pupils, so I have little to complain about in that department.

My own great interest is in teaching the students to jump. My predecessor concentrated mostly on the kind of riding skill that would be necessary in wartime. My own feelings are that there is probably little chance of those skills being needed in the future I see before us. Our Citizen King has not only provided us with a noble and worthy successor in the Duke of Orléans, but there has just been a new prince born to Ferdinand and his German duchess. This would seem to give us three generations of kings that we can depend upon, and the throne seems ensured. The Bonapartists are always hiding out in some nearby country or other, but it is difficult to imagine that there can be any real enthusiasm for them. Perhaps if the King of Rome *[The King of Rome was the infant son of Napoleon the First, by his second wife, the Austrian princess Marie-Louise. He was also known as L'Aiglon (The Eaglet). He was to die in Vienna mysteriously in his early twenties.]* hadn't died in his exile in Vienna there could be some real interest, but otherwise, it seems unlikely. How do you feel about the possibilities that he was poisoned? The flamboyance of the past fifty years in France makes nothing impossible.

I am pleased to report that I have made the very pleasant acquaintance of a gentleman in the nearby town of Saint Marc, whom I met in a café there. He is a gentleman of leisure of the name of Contant, related to some good families here I gather, who is very well read and an excellent conversationalist. He tells me that he is not at all the indolent fellow he might seem as he has already produced five children and sees no end in sight. He explained that he spends a good deal of time at the café because, although it is a noisy place, it is a haven of peace in comparison to his own home. He is an amusing chap and I'm sure I will see more of him.

As for female acquaintanceship here in Terrassée, we have quite a pretty maid here in this residence I have chosen, and her bedroom, in fact, is directly above mine. There is a servants' staircase that descends directly behind my room that leads down into the storage rooms to the rear as well as up to her room. We shall see in the near future if there is some true function for this staircase other than for her to come in to make up my bed and empty my chamber pot.

I have also sighted a very lovely married lady at the village church. Churchgoing is an essential part of finding women, as you well know. This lady has a withdrawn manner, but she is tall, dark-haired with a lovely figure and an appealing face. There is something a bit Mediterranean about her, which pleased me. I need not explain that to you. She is always accompanied by her husband, a very serious-looking kind of person, and I overheard the priest address her as Countess as she was leaving the church last Sunday. All of this fires the imagination, don't you think?

I remain, as always, your devoted servant and faithful cousin,

Gilles de Thorigny

# Chapter 27
## Third Letter
## from Gilles de Thorigny

15 November 1838

My Dear Cousin Gustave,

What a quick reply to my letter of not even three weeks ago. Of course you are in Paris, which is not the end of the world. And I suspect that you have little to do, waiting as you are for some kind of military action to engage you, as I am myself. And undoubtedly thinking, as I do, that it is quite unlikely.

I think we were both lucky to have had our training at the School of Versailles under the Viscount d'Abzac. Though we were in the last class, I believe the training we received was far superior to that now being given under the Count d'Aure at Saumur. I rode over there while the abbey school was closed last week because of a bout of measles and saw what I considered were far too many innovations. There is a certain amount of "forcing" of the horse in the kind of training being given there that I cannot agree with.

When I returned here to the reopened school I gave my students quite a stirring little lecture. I told them, which I so firmly believe and I'm sure with which you agree, "The horse is the best judge of a good rider, not the observer. If the horse has a high opinion of the rider he will allow himself to be guided. If not, he will resist." The boys who have their own horses here are the lucky ones as they can establish a personal relationship, but I warned them not to think of their horse as though he or she was another person. I told my students, " Your horse does not have an intelligence. Your horse cannot, therefore, analyze, deduct, or correct. On the other hand, your horse has an extraordinary memory. And that is what you must work with." Doesn't that sound good? I am not at all sure but what I thought of that myself. Perhaps we heard that in our training. But if that is true I have suppressed it and now firmly believe that I have thought of it myself. If I am wrong, please do me the favor of not telling me.

It sounds as though you have found a very fetching little friend in Paris. Of course, since she is not someone's wife it will result in costing you some money, but that is perhaps the best course to take. It is yours and there when you wish to have it, although there is a certain amount of excitement and pleasure in having forbidden pleasures and not at all being sure when you are going to have them.

I have made very little progress with the pretty maid Marie-Therese, who is in my bedroom every day when I am out but never there when I am in. I suggested that I might come to visit her in her room some evening, which suggestion she rebuffed immediately. "Oh, no, sir, that would be quite incorrect," she replied. Somehow suggesting that she was not good enough for me to come a visiting.

I have made some progress with the handsome Countess, however. I encountered her on the street of the village with her maid, who, I might add, is a pretty little lady herself. I introduced myself with the greatest Parisian style that I could muster and told her that I had the pleasure of being an acquaintance of her brother-in-law in Saint Marc. She was quite pleasant and laughed and said that I was actually more fortunate than herself as she had never had the pleasure of meeting her brother-in-law. When I protested that he was the most splendid of fellows and that she must meet him as Saint Marc was so close, she replied, without being disdainful in any way, "In some ways." I would gather there has been some kind of falling out between her husband, the Count, and his overbreeding brother. We went our ways with protestations of pleasure at making each other's acquaintance, but the Countess is an intelligent woman. I think she saw through my game immediately. I believe she must be only a few years older than myself but she has no jeune-fille manners about her. Which is good. It is so terribly vulgar on mature women those little grimaces and fingers in the curls and in the corner of the mouth. That is not at all the style of our Countess.

When I returned to the house Marie-Therese was on the stoop, and I asked her what she knew of the Countess. She looked a bit jealous, I must admit. She told me the Countess was not long ago come to the Chateau Le Rivage to the northwest of the village toward Chaumont. She has very recently lost a child as the result of a fall from a horse. She is devout and in very regular attendance at the village church. I told her that the Countess had said she had never met her brother-in-law, who lived so nearby in Saint Marc. Marie-Therese replied, "Oh, that wouldn't be possible." But would say no more.

My next move on this ever-more-interesting chessboard will be to introduce the Countess to her brother-in-law. They will then become friendly and I will be the go-between, which will place me in a position to reap the benefit of the Countess's appreciation. As with any game of this kind, one cannot see the next ploy until the present one is completed. No one understands this better than yourself.

And now I must leave you. The gray skies and the blowing leaves of little Terrassée look much less bleak to me today. There will certainly be much to amuse me in the winter months ahead.

With all my never-ending dedication to you, my dear cousin,

Gilles de Thorigny

**Chapter 28**
**Fourth Letter**
**from Gilles de Thorigny**


15 December 1838

My Dear Cousin,

Are these letters from this lost little hamlet amusing you? I suppose I envy you your worldly life in Paris and perhaps hope to make you a little jealous that there are other little worlds of intrigue and emotion and plotting. A world that has its charms, even if it is far from the excitement of Paris.

I think I have a very good plan that has already been well set afoot. I have made the acquaintance of our mayor in the village of Terrassée, a certain Maitre Hibou. He is of a local good family that have been the lawyers in this town for several generations. His wife, who is not from this part of the country but hails from Normandy, feels herself somewhat above the citizens of this small town. She has actually been to Mont Saint Michel. Can you imagine? We have met at several small parties and teas given here and each time she regales me once again with how exciting it was to cross over to that religious hilltop while the tides were low and how fearful she was that there might be an unexpectedly early return of the tide and that her party and she might be swept out to sea. She is a not at all bad-looking blonde, and I rather enjoy listening to the same story each time we meet. At the last afternoon tea I suggested that she might like to meet the Countess Contant de Cazas as a person truly worth knowing here in our rather far-flung world. This, of course, captured her attention. I told her I was fortunate enough to actually have the acquaintance of the Countess, which is factually true. And that perhaps I could arrange a small get-together in the salon of the house where I am residing and that the Countess might agree to attend.

My plan, of course, is to also invite the Countess's brother-in-law, whom I know she would like very much to meet, whereas I know she would not have the slightest desire to meet the somewhat less-than-interesting Madame Hibou, blonde as she is.

I have couched everything in terms of a social afternoon to celebrate Christmas. I discussed the possibility of a gathering with my landlord, who is only too happy to let me spend the money for a party, which our little maid, Marie-Therese, will arrange for the most part with the help of his wife. Of course, his wife and he must be in attendance, but there is no help for that. I wish to have a goodly number of people so that the Countess is not overly suspicious that I have created this for the sole purpose of her meeting her own relatives. And, of course, I wish to allay all suspicion that it is solely to advance my own acquaintanceship with her.

The party is to be next Saturday so that she may combine attendance with her usual weekly sortie into Terrassée for her small errands and purchases. We met yesterday. I, of course, laying wait in the café at the crossroads but appearing to be quite casually walking in the street, and I asked her if she might be able to stop for a short while the next Saturday. I told her that her brother-in-law would be in attendance. I also added that it was not that I expect that she would find the townspeople of my acquaintance very fascinating but that as the chatelaine of Le Rivage, the more important citizens would like to meet her and it was in some way her duty. She laughed when I told her this and agreed that she would come but would not be able to stay for very long and that unfortunately her husband would not be coming with her because of all the requirements at the chateau of his time and attention before winter truly set in. It is my opinion that she in no way wished her husband to know that she is planning to meet his younger brother and will probably not even mention the party to him. And so the plot thickens, and very nicely.

An added amusing note is that I believe our pretty little household maid will undoubtedly become jealous, as women are so quick to see through our little stratagems. Even simple little household maids.

My friend, Monsieur Contant, in Saint Marc is only too happy to attend, although he says his wife will not, and I have also invited the other instructors at the abbey and the wives of those few who are married. As many of the instructors are priests, my little gathering will be above reproach, even should the Countess decide to discuss it later with her husband. I know that you will be wanting to know the results of these festivities, and I will report to you shortly thereafter. To be amusing, life only needs some imagination directed at it. Don't you agree?

Please believe that I am your devoted cousin and servant,

Gilles

**Chapter 29**
**Fifth Letter**
**from Gilles de Thorigny**


5 January 1839

My Dear Cousin,

I rush to put pen to paper to tell you about my amusing holiday contretemps. Before I do, I hope that you had the most joyous of Christmases and the best of all possible New Year's celebrations.

My own was quite an unusual event. I had planned a holiday fete using the reception room to the large house I am living in, primarily to take the opportunity of introducing the Comtesse Contant de Cazas to her own brother-in-law and his wife. I had imagined a blazing fire, a large bowl of grog, a local fiddler, and some prancing and dancing and the everlasting gratitude of the Comtesse to be expressed in who knows how many ways.

I had delivered an invitation by passing it to the Countess's maid when I saw her in the streets of the village. The next day we encountered each other again, and she told me that since it was an afternoon party that the Countess felt that she could convince the Count to drop by with her as they visited other friends in the village on a round of Christmas visits. I was then forced to tell her that Monsieur and Madame Contant from St. Marc would also be present. She is a quick young woman, and I think sees through my stratagems in a way her mistress so far has not. She said she would relay the message.

There was no reply, and I had none until the afternoon before the party, when all foodstuffs and drinks had been laid in and all guests invited. The Countess and herself and her maid in their carriage were at the intersection of the village and the Countess beckoned to me. "I have thought greatly about your kind invitation, and I know that it has been extended with only the best intentions, but I feel any attempts at reconciliation between my husband and his brother should not take place in such a public atmosphere. I think often our pride does not allow us to bend when we are being observed." I bowed in acquiescence although burning at the expenditure I had gone to.

She then added, "To make it up to you for any disappointment I will gladly stop by their home on my next shopping expedition to St. Marc. And hopefully you will be there, also." One of the finest ladies of Paris could not have arranged things more smoothly. I believe she feels something for me. There will be more news soon, I hope.

Your devoted cousin,

Gilles de Thorigny

*D. D. Abercrombie note:* There were, however, no further letters from Gilles de Thorigny to his cousin on this subject. The few others made no mention of the Countess and only spoke of army affairs and the possibility of his rejoining his unit, which he seems to have had no encouragement about.

# Chapter 30
## More from D. D.
## Abercrombie's Journal



My friend D. D Abercrombie did not keep a true diary. She kept a journal into which she taped pictures from newspapers and magazines, wrote quotes from books and magazine articles she was reading, and occasionally wrote notes on her thoughts. During the period of her research of the Comtesse she wrote at greater length, as though wanting to create connective material for the letters and other material she was copying and notating.


Yesterday I had an unusual call from the librarian at the military museum in Paris. She seemed quite interested in my project and was quite friendly. How curious the French are. When I visited the library she was very cool and seemed to be barely controlling an active dislike for me. I think the French do this upon meeting someone new just in case that person will dislike them. And then they can never be rebuffed. They have expressed their dislike first.

The librarian was calling to say my interest had led her to do a routine check on General de Thorigny's papers, just to verify that all was in order.  (More likely to make sure I hadn't stolen anything.) She had discovered another group of letters filed under the name of Gilles de Thorigny. They were not from Gilles de Thorigny but were in female handwriting and folded neatly in an embroidered silk stocking. They had evidently been put in an adjacent file by another earlier librarian who must have thought they were not directly pertinent to General de Thorigny's bequest. Would I be interested in seeing them?

Of course I was and, of course, although I was willing to come to Paris the next day that would not be convenient for her as it was her day off and she was taking her daughter to the circus. (How unusually intimate for a Frenchwoman to tell this to another woman she scarcely knew. And who would have thought she was young enough to have daughter of an age to still enjoy the circus? No father probably. French women had fatherless children years before it became fashionable.)

We agreed on Friday, and I took an early train. I was sure she must have stumbled upon letters from Catherine to Gilles. They had to be. Of course, they could be letters from some other woman to him. I had to hold my emotions in check to that degree.

Mme. Deneuve, she has the same last name as the famous French film star, showed me into the research room and proudly gestured toward a library tray waiting for me on the table. A small pale green silk package with what looked like tiny pink embroidered roses decorating it lay there. "You may unwrap it," she said. I did. "It's well preserved. Not too fragile." Her smile was that of a proud mother watching her delighted child receive her first Christmas present. And then she swept away without a noise.

I sat down and stared at the little package. It was so rare and precious to me. Was I going to be disappointed? As gently as I could, I unwrapped what turned out to be a stocking, as Mme. Deneuve had said, which had been wrapped around the letters within. It was quite long and had been exquisitely knitted on what must have been tiny, slender needles. It was of pale green silk. The color was still quite fresh. The clock design that ran up one side was of pink roses and darker green leaves, embroidered with an equally tiny stitch. This one stocking alone must have required many hours of work. I could imagine some woman somewhere, her hair in a bun, sitting in a window, slowly, slowly creating this exquisite covering for another woman's leg, to be seen for just a moment as a skirt was lifted to mount into a carriage or descend a staircase. There was another world in this stocking.

The letters were small and still all in their envelopes. The envelopes were somewhat browned along their edges but not overly brittle. They were of a very heavy, rich paper, still smooth and quite pliable. I counted. There were seven of them.

Gingerly, I picked up the top one. There was no name or address on it. It had been sealed with sealing wax and the broken seal was too indistinct for me to make out any details. The seal seemed to be a shape rather than initials. The letter was brief and curiously, was left unsigned.


Dear Monsieur de Thorigny,

I would like to express my great pleasure at the opportunity you gave me to meet my brother-in-law and his wife Thursday last at your home.

I'm sure you realize that the situation was irregular, and my husband does not yet know this meeting has taken place. However, I believe the circumstances were entirely innocent and it is, of course, my dearest wish that these two brothers repair their differences and become friends again. Your kind gesture may very well be the first step in leading to this happy event.

May I add that I found my new brother's consort an intelligent and obviously loving spouse, entirely devoted to her husband's welfare and happiness, which is everything one could wish. I see no reason why she and I should not be friends one day.

Thank you for your kind interest in our family's happiness.


There this letter ends. The handwriting is the beautiful script of all the educated people of the early part of the nineteenth century, so perfect and also so identical that it is virtually impossible to seek out any individual quirks and personality revelations.

However, I could compare it to the Comtesse's letters to her aunt, which are in my possession. That is, if my new friend the librarian can arrange to make copies.

Once I had read the others I knew this was an absolute necessity, or I have to return to painstakingly copy each of them out. So much emotion had been crushed into these letters that the small packet almost pulsed beneath my hand.

Fortunately, Annette Deneuve (so much had our friendship advanced) said she could arrange to have them photographed and would have copies sent to me as quickly as possible. She inquired gently if I was writing a book. "I don't know. I don't think so," I told her. "I'm just curious."

"Curiosity is such an excellent quality," she said, smiling at me as though I had become more recognizable to her. More French.

## Chapter 31
## The Abercrombie
## Journal Continues

Countess Catherine' affair with the riding instructor must have ignited like a flash of gunpowder, as her second letter clearly indicates that they have had a sexual consummation. After her first prim letter, she must have accepted visiting him in his room and fallen directly into his arms. The term she uses to address him in her letters, "Mon Grand Cheri," may indicate that he was a tall, large man, or the "Grand" may indicate the scale of her passion for him. I have translated it as "My Great Love" although "My Big Darling" would be a more contemporary translation.

My Great Love,
What am I able to say to you after our encounter yesterday other than that I have passed from a world of well controlled gloom to one of radiant light.

Only a few days ago I looked down the long years to come with a saddened patience, ready to repeat endlessly the meaningless action of rising, dressing, eating, visiting neighbors, shopping—with no interest in any of it. I had resigned myself to the path the Lord had assigned to me.

And then suddenly, like Apollo in his chariot, only on horseback in this case, you descended from the heavens and swept me off in your arms. I don't think it could have happened if you were not blond. And I was convinced of it as I looked up and saw your halo of hair hovering over me in the light filtering through the window. Your chest and arms as they pressed down upon me were like the marble of a statue, made rosy and warm with your blood coursing within.

I have never experienced intimacy in the daylight before and never so stripped of all the appurtenances of clothing, with shoes and stockings and all clothing cast aside. It was a revelation. I have never seen my husband as completely as I have seen you. Nor has he ever seen me as you have seen me. Does this not then in some way make us a couple as must have existed in antiquity? Daphnis and Chloe perhaps. I would not dare to go so far as to suggest Venus and Apollo, although your beauty could easily have served one of the great Greek sculptors. Praxiteles perhaps.

I will not sign this letter, and I have adjusted my handwriting so as to not be easily identified as my own in case this letter should one day go astray. Although I have no experience in this venturing outside the structure and strictures of my everyday life, I have read many novels, and I do not wish to hurl myself too completely into the void. At least not yet.

Your Angel


**Translator's note:**
"Mon Ange" is still frequently heard in contemporary France, and its only translation would be "my angel." Again, I remind myself and anyone who may read this, it is only a highly educated guess that these letters are from Catherine.

From D. D. Abercrombie's Journal:
I have spent some time comparing the letters written by the Comtesse to her aunt and the letters from the estate of General de Thorigny written to his cousin. Since handwriting was so extremely uniform in this period, the back-handing of the love letters is not very extreme but does look entirely different from the correspondence to Catherine's aunt.

There are occasional great similarities in the capital "E" and the letters "G" and "J," which are difficult to transform in French, but probably in comparison with much correspondence of many different people of the era would result in the same conclusions. The quill pen allowed for a very limited degree of variation in handwriting.

For me, the same leads me to draw final conclusions. The fact that the letter paper is the same leads me to draw more final conclusions. But then again, available writing paper of this time may have been limited and very similar, also. It is thick paper, and the process for creating it was largely only used for newspapers. The gentry didn't think it was good enough to use for correspondence. Many still don't. I must research this and see what I can find out about writing paper in the early nineteenth century.

## Chapter 32
## The Third Letter
## from Catherine to Gilles

My Great Love,

My little cat is lying on my desk as I write to you. She stared at me with her great vertical eyes as though to ask me a question. Do I know what I am doing? Do I know where I am going? Am I the same person that she saw leaving this room only this morning? The answer to all these questions is "no."

I can never be the same person that I was before we met. Nor can my life ever be the same. My life on the other side was so normal, so expected, so reassuring. I knew where it was going and nothing about me suggested that it should be otherwise. And then you appeared like the God of the Sun, and I realized that there is a great deal more to life than I have ever understood or expected. How do you feel as you read this? Is this exactly the kind of thing every silly woman writes to the man she should not love?

You have introduced me to the life of the body which I believe has nothing to do with the life of the mind. Our minds scarcely know each other, you must agree with this. We have rarely spoken of anything serious. But our bodies seem to know each other very well. Is it not something like a horse and its rider? The rider, the mind, guides the horse this way and that, but has no real understanding of how the horse feels. And then suddenly the horse runs away. Is the rider always in peril? Or is it perhaps what the rider has been longing for? It is not the rider who now makes the decisions; it is the horse.

You, of course, must be more aware of this as the horse and the riding of it is your métier. Do you ever feel this way? Or are you perhaps still very much in command of your horse as you plunge into my body and I, lying beneath you, am the horse that has run away and lost its senses. However it is, I now only wait until the moment is propitious that I can once again slip through the little staircase door into your room. When will that be?

(D. D. Abercrombie note: There is no signature.)

**Chapter 33**
**The Fourth Letter**
**from the Comtesse**
**Catherine to Gilles**
**De Thorigny**


Editor's note:

D. D. Abercrombie was obviously trying to correlate the letters of Comtesse Catherine to her aunt that had newly arrived in her hands with the letters to Gilles de Thorigny, which she was yet to be assured were from the Comtesse. Her own notes were not profuse in her journal, but she carefully placed her translations in the journal in an order I feel sure was deliberate.


My Great Love, (The opening of this letter is "Mon Grand Amour," unlike the other letter so it has been translated differently here.)

How unfortunate it is that we are not able to hold our emotions at such a pitch that we cannot remain in each other's arms twenty-four hours of every day. For when I am with you I feel that it would be entirely possible. I imagine that I could just disappear from the world altogether. No one would know where I had gone, and would they even notice my absence or wonder where I disappeared? And would they think of looking in your bed? I have become so bold. I wish that it had not been necessary to admit my maid to my confidences, but there truly has been no other way I could come and see you without arousing suspicions. I am well aware that every eye in a small village is open to my irregularity. Fortunately, my maid's mother lives just around the corner from you and is confined to her bed, so that I can pass an hour or so in her house come an afternoon, under the guise of bringing company to the ill.

I should feel guilt at the farce of my slipping directly down her hallway and out the side door that leads into the same courtyard where your staircase ascends. In less than a minute I am upstairs and in your room. Certainly someone in an upper room living on the courtyard will notice one day and rumors will begin to fly. Do you suppose that my claim that I am in the courtyard only to use le petit coin will be believed if I am ever questioned?


(D. D. Abercrombie note: I have retained le petit coin for toilet as it is a rural expression whose literal translation, "the little corner," is not very meaningful.)


I'm sure the word "reckless" should be used to describe my behavior, but it does not seem or feel in any way careless or uncontrolled. It is more like a fleck of metal being called back to its magnet.

I understand that your knowledge of women is far greater than my knowledge of men, but even so, my sense of a strong current of emotion flowing between us is hopefully as unique for you as it is for me. This is not something commonplace that is happening between us, and it can no more be denied, in my opinion than the spring floods that overflow the banks of the Loire River. Who can turn the tides and the floods?

The last time that we were together as you held me in your arms you said, "This must be love for us to be back together in each other's arms having just made love." That I hold in my heart like a lodestar, guiding me in this journey that leads me into an unseeable void.

And now I must return to my other life, loving you even more because it is not possible to remain in your arms all of every day.

Your Angel

## Chapter 34
## The Fifth Letter from the
## Comtesse Catherine
## to Gilles de Thorigny


My Dear, My Dear, My Dear, My Dear, Since my maid is venturing into the village to search for sewing thread, I am sending this note with her to be slipped under your door. The necessity of taking her into my confidence had made me unhappy for a number of reasons, but we have become something like close friends. Or perhaps it is the complicity of prisoners. She too feels that she is trapped in a way in her life at the chateau.

As for my own escape, it can only be into my dreams. Since my maid's mother has recovered, there is little excuse for me to visit her, and the last time I did, you were unable to be in your room so our meeting in that manner is no longer possible. I am planning to be near the hunting lodge where the road from Terrassée intersects with the road from St. Marc on its way to Chaumont at about three o'clock in the afternoon. Perhaps if you can escape your students it would be possible for us to encounter each other there. Almost by chance. I will be riding for several hours, and I will hover near the lodge for about half an hour. More than that would seem peculiar should other riders be out and about that day.

I remain in hopes of seeing you at that time.

The A.


D. D. Abercrombie note:

Obviously, the relationship between the Countess and her riding instructor-lover was taking a new turn at the time of this letter. I would estimate that the Countess had kept a rendezvous at Gilles's room that he had failed to attend. Perhaps he was not keeping in touch with notes, such as she was sending him. None of the Countess's notes are dated, but Gilles de Thorigny seems to have kept them in the order in which he received them.

In my own imagining, Gilles de Thorigny has made his conquest of the Countess and is not wishing to jeopardize his position at the abbey school by running off with her. Without family money and his only important contact being his cousin in the army, he was fortunate to have the position he had as riding instructor in one of France's most prestigious schools.

Perhaps none of this is true. Perhaps he was madly in love with Catherine and wished to leave Terrassée with her. But there would have been very little for them once they had left. They would have had to live in poverty somewhere. The Countess would have been disgraced. Divorce and remarriage would have been unlikely. The world of George Sand allowed such things, but these were wealthy women pairing off with famous artists like Chopin and Liszt or women who left their husbands for other wealthy men to live in luxuriousness as concubines.

It should be added that Catherine, in her letter, does not seem to have the calculating character of many of these women either. She seems to have not been in love before meeting Gilles de Thorigny and the experience swept her away, although she was mature enough and wise enough to realize it had little hope of being anything more than a romantic affair.

As for Gilles de Thorigny, one can not imagine that he was in love or that he was even familiar with feelings of those kind. As a handsome blond womanizer, certainly he was used to being adored. The only great romance of his life was very likely with himself.


**Author's note:**
As my friend D. D. Abercrombie became more enmeshed in the story she was disinterring, her own notes become more voluminous, undoubtedly as the people involved became more and more real for her.

———

**Chapter 35
Sixth Letter from
the Comtesse to Gilles
De Thorigny**

My Great Cavalier,

All my memories of thou are being threaded together so that sometime when I am old I can run them through my head, much as I handle my rosary bead. One by one they will be held close and carefully examined. And many years from now, they will be as fresh and beautiful as they were at the moment they happened.

As we lay in our bower of green, deep in the forest, what could have been more splendid than your powerful body holding me close? Adam and Eve in Eden must have felt the same joy, the same ecstasy. It was like the dawn of the world. If a child were to be born of our union in that tiny grove, how beautiful he would be. The sunlight falling like golden coins around us, the branches weaving together overhead, moving gently in the soft, southern wind. And then thou were lost within me, your body soaring against the broken rays of the sun, then falling back upon me as though to sink into the earth itself, carrying me with thou into deep oblivion. Whatever may happen in our lives, I would not want to have lived and not known this kind of exaltation. And for this, I will always have thou to thank, my golden god, my heavenly warrior.

And though we were both naked, I believe that in the openness of my heart, I was nakeder than thou.

And now, adieu. When we meet again I cannot guess. My maid slips out the door at this moment on her way to mass. She will leave this under your door.

From the woman you have made into . . . an Angel.

D. D. Abercrombie note

After sleeping with Gilles de Thorigny the Countess begin using "tu" in her notes, the familiar form of "you" which is customary in France. In this letter, I have translated using "thou" and "thine" only because of the beauty of her prose.

How much more explosive and monumental sex was in those days when so much was forbidden and so much was impossible. What a great life-shaking experience her love for Gilles de Thorigny was for the Countess, whereas in our own time it would have been conducted in some second-rate motel whose very atmosphere makes it unimportant and something of which to be ashamed.

**Chapter 36**
**The Seventh Letter**
**from the Comtesse**


My Dear Cavalier, My Dear Saint George, How heartbreaking our last meeting began! When you suddenly appeared at the chateau to tell me that you were leaving for the war in Spain. How impossible it was for me to accept this news. And then the joyous resolution that I will go with you. What madness! What sanity!

How can I write more when my heart is so full? How can I even think when my head is so full of thoughts about my new life to come? A life freed of the burden of my daily existence.

No more will I be like a prisoner, trudging around the same well-worn path of duties. To arise, to dress, to discuss what will be served for meals with the cook, who cares nothing at all for my requests or suggestions but continues to cook the same dreary round of beef and fowl. The little trips into the village, the polite little visits to neighbors who were born boring, who live boringly, and will remain boring all their lives. And surely they will die in the most boring of ways. And are so smugly content that they have managed boring little lives without a moment's excitement or irregularity.

Now I depart from all that, like a balloon that has escaped its tether. A balloon that will float higher and higher where the sun shines more brightly, where the breezes are stronger, where the clouds pile higher and higher, waiting only for the gods to alight upon them.

To return to earth, Minette and I are leaving the house at midnight. We will walk directly across the fields to St. Marc, which is not so very long a walk when one travels off the road. It will certainly not take us more than two hours. I will go directly to my brother-in-law's house, where they will be waiting. Minette will return by herself to the chateau. She says she is not afraid to do this, and accompanying me I will be able to depart with two small valises, providing me with an adequate if simple wardrobe.

I am quite prepared to dress myself and dress my own hair. I know how to do this, and you will be surprised how hardy a traveler I can be. Like "Paul and Virginie" we will set off into our new lives together, like pioneers in the American wilderness.

Oh, my great darling, I always knew that life was more than this endless round of actions that one is expected to make, like some mechanical doll. And it is you who has opened the door for me. I stand on the threshold now, looking over the sunlit plains, reaching toward an endless horizon. How happy we will be, for whatever happens to us, wherever we are, we will be together.

Your angel who is about to enter heaven,


Catherine



D. D. Abercrombie notes:

Whatever happened? What an amazing letter! From my end of this historical tunnel, I can only look back and be heartsick that whatever the Comtesse hoped for in her great love for Gilles de Thorigny, it never occurred—because I know that she remained at the chateau for the rest of her life, repeating all those mechanical little activities she hoped to escape from.

My imagination races. Catherine waiting through the night for her lover who never appears, after a very long walk across the dark fields. Where was the moon that night? I can probably find out approximately. Carrying a heavy valise made of carpet, her maid at her side with another valise, their skirts scuffing over the furrows.

And as dawn arrives with no lover and no escape she must return in humiliation to the chateau. What does she say? How does she explain? Does she even try to? Or does she simply go to her room and resume her life as though nothing had happened?

Or did a messenger come before she ever set out for that long walk to St. Marc. Did the little maid from Gilles's boarding house slip out with a message and run to the chateau to tell her there would be no departure?

My own romantic imagination tells me that Gilles de Thorigny was killed and buried in my cave at Passage du Salut. Someone at the abbey school was probably told by him that he was leaving so there was no search for him in the village. But what about his horse and his personal belongings? What of them? How were they dispersed?

And what did Catherine think? All she knew was that he disappeared. Did she suspect the Comte? Did she think he had simply walked out on her? It is so strange that I, D. D. Abercrombie, know that someone was buried in the cave, and no one then knew. The Comtesse lived all her life wondering what became of the man she loved, and now, so many years later when it can matter to no one anymore, I know. Or do I? I must remember that. This has all become so real to me and yet much of this history I hold in my mind may very well be fiction that I am imagining, that I am creating.

But it would not be fictional to imagine that the Comtesse screamed and cried in the night in her bedroom at the chateau. Her shadow jerking and falling against the walls in the flickering light of a single candle as her maid tries to console her.

I imagine Catherine composing herself by dawn, either as a married woman betrayed or as a woman whose lover has been killed. Either way, Catherine must have been a woman made of strong stuff. She knew she had no role now except as the Comte's wife. The endless days would be clicking by now all the way to the end of her life. The door had been slammed shut on the vista of the golden plains, under a bright blue sky filled with the low-lying fluffy clouds that are always present in the summer skies of the Touraine. Now there will be only the endless gray rooms of routine. And the luxury that will accompany her empty life.

**Chapter 37**
**A Brief Letter to Her**
**Aunt from Catherine**


13 March 1839

My Dear Aunt,

What can I tell you about my present life here at the Chateau Le Rivage as spring approaches? Though I have now been here almost two years, it seems as though I have just recently arrived. I don't seem to have really noticed that the spring flowers were so vivid in color, that the colors were so varied and that a faint haze of green lines every tree limb, every hilltop. This is a spring that seems full of promise which, considering the sadness that has been encountered in this plain that is called a valley but is nothing of the sort, should be very good news to your ears.

Sorry that I have nothing more to say except that everything is all the same, and yet everything is different. And that I have learned that no one is whom they seem.

Your obedient niece,

Catherine

# Chapter 38
## The Obituary of
## the Comtesse


D. D. Abercrombie note:

After reading the last letter of the Comtesse, I knew it would be unlikely for me to find any remainders of personal witnessing of those days. Even if there were more letters to the Comtesse's aunt to be found, they would only be filled with the banalities of the repetitive rhythms of her life at the chateau. I decided to go to the other end of her life and read what was said of her at the close of her days. Surely the newspaper in Blois would have had an obituary.

I called the offices of the Nouvelle République and asked how long they had been published and was told since 1875. But there had been a predecessor newspaper, Le Courrier du Val de Loire, all of whose files had been transferred to microfilm in the 1950s. If I wished to come into their offices I could review these films at any time and at no charge. Occasionally in France one stumbles upon some little niche where things have not been unnecessarily bureaucratized and made difficult, only to give some petty bureaucrats something to do.

A fresh, pretty young secretary greeted me at the offices of the Nouvelle République and seemed to remember my call. Probably few people want to use the paper's microfilm services.

Bernard, Comte Contant de Cazas

Since I knew the date of the Comtesse's death to be May 1871, I asked for films on the two-week period following. I found the obituary easily as it was then, as it is now, a weekly paper. The obituary was in the first edition after her death. In a heavy black border and larger than any of the other obituaries that surrounded it, it was simple to locate. It read:

It is with great sorrow and regret that the Comte Contant de Cazas announces the departure of his mother Catherine, Comtesse Contant de Cazas. Now she is among the angels where she so rightly belongs as she passed her days among us as a spirit from another realm who came to earth to show us how to live. The Comtesse was born at the Chateau de Cazas near Aix-en-Provence in 1811. She became the bride of Bernard, Comte Contant de Cazas in 1838. Her son, the present Comte Contant de Cazas, was born in 1840. The late Comte Contant de Cazas, her husband, was deceased in 1865.

All the residents of the region will remember her good
works, her instituting of a school for young girls in Terrassée, and
her contribution of the chapel of Sainte Catherine to the church

Gilles de Thorigny

of Terrassée.  Always devout, she was noted for her daily
attendance at mass in the chapel built upon the grounds of the
Chateau Le Rivage for her own use.

    While at the newspaper I also asked to see the edition of the week of the death of her son, the Comte Gilles. His obituary promptly turned up in the edition published the week after his death, the date of which I had noted from his tombstone. I wanted to see if his birth date was included, as his tombstone only held the year. It was there. December 20, 1840. Clearly, the Comtesse had been pregnant at the time of her lover's disappearance. It seems obvious to me that Gilles de Thorigny was the father of her child. She had never had other children. There is much here to think about.

# Chapter 39
## The Angels

From D. D. Abercrombie's Journal:

I had a dream last night I must tell you about. A dream that I have had difficulty recovering, as though my subconscious hinted at something, and then later regretted it.

I had a dream of angels. The male angel was called Cleliel. That's something in itself, isn't it? That there are angels of both sexes. Cleliel was tall and blond and looked very much like the handsomest blond man I have ever known. Cleliel was very busy in constructing a kind of tree form with found objects, all of which had to be crystalline and silvery. He was busily hanging silver cigarette lighters, strings of rhinestone beads, bits of silver paper, many unidentifiable objects which all glittered and shone as they trembled slightly, from the wire form that resembled a Christmas tree. Cleliel was dressed in a tight-fitting white sailor uniform with a sailor hat pushed back on his blond hair.

His female counterpoint was named Liliel. I remember very little of Liliel except that she was also blonde and tall and in white. At one point, Cleliel, who so resembled a blond male friend who is resolutely heterosexual, perched himself on a barstool at a silvery bar that was in the room and pushed his white-clad buttocks off the back of it in a very provocative way. Have you ever seen the homoerotic drawings of Tom of Finland? It was like that.

I tell you all this because perhaps this what has become of the Countess Catherine and her love, Gilles de Thorigny. Perhaps the forces that seem to be provoking me to gather material on their lives so long ago are trying to give me some information about what happens in the lives of the angels, however fragmentary. Perhaps not.

## Chapter 40
## La Gardienne


From D. D. Abercrombie's Journal:

I have a housekeeper. Well, not really. I guess she is what the French would call a gardienne. She does not clean. The cleaning lady is someone else, Madame Lauron. My gardienne comes by daily when I am absent to check the mail and to see that no lights have been left on and I suppose to be sure that no one has ransacked the house during the night. It has happened. In St. Marc a large house on the edge of town had its furniture stolen while the owners were in Paris. They caught the culprits. It was the owner of the local pastry shop and his mother-in-law. The next day I happened to be in that shop. His wife, daughter of the co-thief, stood behind the counter calm and stony-faced as always. A few days later the shop was closed. Hubby and Mommy were off to prison.

So my gardienne had reason to be on guard, even though I was situated between the priest's residence and the hairdresser. One never could tell. My gardienne's name is Monique, although I refer to her as Madame Trian. Were I to call her Monique it would lower her in her own esteem vis-à-vis an employer. Particularly an American one. The French Revolution did have certain effects. So I, of course, wind up never using her first or second name when speaking to her directly. She calls me Madame D. D. She does pronounce it the American way. Perhaps she thinks it's spelled Didi. That would come out correctly in French.

Monique Trian is small and blonde and chirpy and tough as an old boot. She has a large, dark, slow-moving husband a good bit younger than herself. I think they are quite happy together.

I have known her quite a few years now. She found Madame Lauron for me, who used to clean. Now I clean myself. With Madame Lauron the wreckage was horrific. The ravaging of china statuettes, glass dishes, and voile curtains was monumental. A large terra-cotta statuette I turned to the wall to avoid damage she even managed to reach a dust mop behind and knock a toe off. And then she vacuumed the toe up so it was gone forever. Even staircase railings were torn loose. Madame Lauron did not know her own strength. And her cleaning technique was volcanic. Or hurricane-like, Force-10. So when she announced that she must retire to care for the children of her twin daughters I received the news without regret.

Among Madame Monique's other duties were to pay bills for me if I was absent for long periods, to gather workmen to repair the flyaway roof tiles, the ever-collapsing plumbing, the crumbling plaster walls of my seventeenth-century house. What she liked best though, I'm sure, was keeping an eye on things when I was gone.

To enter someone else's home when they are not there is a particular thrill for a French person, I believe. Am I being unfair? I don't think so. The French do not entertain at home very frequently, except for close relatives, so they do not see the interior of each other's homes. Most entertaining is done in public; the home is a deep and secret sanctuary. Which is not to say that I think Monique excavates bureau drawers and delves beneath the beds. The drama would be to enter my bedroom. Perhaps imagining events there that are unlikely to an extreme. And slipping away feeling secretive and knowledgeable. Two emotions the French love.

She stood in the middle of the sitting room as I was writing her check and said, "You are very interested in the de Cazas family, aren't you?"

I looked up and said, "Yes, they seem to be obsessing me." This was a very personal level of conversation for Monique and myself.

"They have obsessed many people for many years," Monique said. "Many generations even." Monique's manner though always cheerful, is brusque. She added, "Unusual to think so often of people one hardly ever sees. The Comtesse and I are the same age, but I have never spoken to her. I only see her in the streets of the village. You have lunch with her. How is she? Nice?" (Actually, Monique said "gentil," which doesn't truly translate as "nice" in my opinion but has overtones of being well brought up, polite, thoughtful of others. To be "gentil" is to be well-bred. In English, the word "gentle" had these qualities at one time, as in the word "gentleman.")

"Yes, of course she is nice," I said. "But somehow, 'nice' isn't a word I'd use for her myself. Perhaps, 'courageous'? Perhaps, 'strong'?" Monique nodded. She didn't budge from her spot in the center of my carpet, bordered with lavender ribbons and purple flowers woven into its edge. "The old Comtesse must have been nice," she said.

"Comtesse Nathalie's mother?" I asked. "I thought she died when the Comtesse was born. Did you know her?"

"No, the first Comtesse. The one who gave the chapel to the church," Monique said.

"The Comtesse Catherine?" I said. Monique nodded her head. She didn't take her eyes off me. She was fishing.

"She seems to have been," I said. "From what I have been able to find out about her." Monique had to have seen the packets of old letters on my desk.

"I have her diary," Monique said. I knew something was going on here. I have been in France long enough to compose myself and not gasp out "What?" or "How?" or "What do you mean?"

I said, excluding as much excitement as I could from my voice, "It must be very interesting."

"I think it is," Monique replied. "Although I don't understand a lot of it. I am not an intellectual."

"But how is it that you have it?" I asked. I was stalling for time. Something was definitely afoot.

"We have always had it. I was born a Rhetoré, you know. The Rhetorés have been in Terrassée as long as anyone knows. My great-great-grandmother was the first Comtesse's maid."

"She was Minette?" I said.

———

136

"I suppose so. Her name was Marie-Anne. I never saw her, of course, but my mother said that when she was a very small girl she remembered sitting on her lap. And she had very soft hands. She had been a lady's maid. She had never worked in the fields."

"And the Comtesse gave her her diary?" I asked.

"I think that she probably took it when the Comtesse died," Monique said. "It was a personal diary. No one in the family saw it until my great-great-grandmother died. And my grandmother kept it very private. I didn't know about it until my own mother was very old. She gave it to me then, and I read it, though there is nothing of great interest in it. Though for you, perhaps, there might be."

Suddenly I understood, Monique was definitely not leaving until something had happened. Some transaction was underway. We were like two people playing "Blindman's Bluff," blindly reaching out to see what the other would do.

I said, "I'd love to see it, Monique." I used her name. Now we were friends. "But it must be very fragile. I pay the library in Paris to copy things. Could I pay you to copy it?"

"How much do you pay them?" Monique said in a business like way.

"Oh, perhaps five hundred francs for about twenty pages," I replied. This was, of course, about twenty times what I actually paid, but I thought I knew what Monique wanted, and it was up to me to find a gracious and undemeaning way to do it. The cost must have seemed very excessive to her also, but she understood what I was offering.

"There are many more than twenty pages," Monique said. "Well, then, I'll have to pay the copying fees even so, won't I?" I said. We both knew we were talking about the same thing now.

"I wouldn't know where to have it copied," Monique said. She was moving now toward the outer edge of the carpet, away from me.

"I can take care of that. I'll be very careful," I told her. "When can you bring it to me?"

"I have it with me," Monique said and went into the front hall where she had left her shopping basket. She returned with a smallish parcel wrapped in brown paper, tied with twine. The paper and twine were old but not as old as the diary must be. Monique placed it on the desk in front of me.

"You can open it," she said.

———

137

I opened the parcel, the twine untying easily. Inside was an oblong-shaped black leather bound book, narrow in the style of a ledger. I opened it. The inside covers were marbleized. The pages inside were covered in the Comtesse's neat, precise handwriting, which was clearly the same as the letters to her aunt, and not that dissimilar from the notes to Gilles de Thorigny. Only about one-third of the book's pages were written in. "How many pages do think there are?" I said.

"Ninety-three," Monique responded. "That's about one hundred," I said. "Do you think two thousand five hundred francs would be all right?" I asked. That would be about five hundred dollars. But worth it.

Monique relaxed. Her face lit up. "That would be very acceptable," she said. "Could I have it in cash?"

When I hesitated she continued, "You can keep the diary and pay me tomorrow. Or even the next day. There is no question but what I trust you completely, Madame D. D."

After Monique left, the little book remained lying on my desk on its brown paper wrapping. I could hardly wait to start reading it.

## Chapter 41
## The Comtesse's Diary


From D. D. Abercrombie's Journal:

Do I even want to waste any time writing about my closing the door behind Monique Trian, going back to my desk, turning on the light as the day was overcast and my north-facing living room was getting dark, and starting to read the Comtesse's diary, right from the beginning? I didn't flip to the back or nitpick here and there. I just sat down at my desk and read. And read and read and read. Although I was used to the early nineteenth-century handwriting it was slow going. Partly because the Comtesse wrote stacking one sentence upon another, as though the book would never be large enough to contain her thoughts, and partly because I didn't want to miss one word.

The Comtesse didn't date her entries except by the year. When it turned she notated it by devoting an entire page to the year number. So there was 1838 when she arrived at the cha teau. And only a few years following. At the end were a few entries that seem to have been entered at random through much of the rest of her life.

The early part of the diary reads much as her letters to her aunt did. She is always cheerful and presents her new life at the cha teau as an adventure. It is something like someone from a Jane Austen or Charlotte Brontë novel might write. It would be impossible to say whether she is shielding the reader from any real intimacy of thought, or whether that kind of intimacy of thought is a modern phenomenon and a woman of that time simply would not have access to her own feelings and be able to express them as we post-Freudians do.

There are a few telling things. I did not translate the entire journal, obviously. (Nor did I ever copy it. I think Monique understood that I never would.) But in what must have been the first months of her marriage she wrote:

My husband sleeps with his arms above his head. This takes up much of the pillow space of the entire bed. I do not mind. I cuddle beside him, tucking myself in below his arm like some pet dog might. He is not too fond of being touched while he is sleeping, but if I wish more space in the bed I can place my hand upon him and he will jolt in his sleep and move away from me. Thus, do negatives becomes positives.


She also writes in a rare confessional moment:

I am truly afraid of horses. They are so enormous, and I can never ignore what it would be like to have one fall on me. I am so frail in proportion to their bulk and strength. And I cannot help but feel that they resent our ability to dominate them and force them to do things that they do not wish to do. Why didn't early men decide to ride cows? They are so much more placid, and there is so much more room to sit sideways upon them. And if they should run away, they would never run very fast. And if you fell, it would not be far.

I fell the other day and my husband made me immediately remount. He said I must or I would be fearful and each day would be harder. I would never tell him that it made me fearful in a way that never goes away. And each day is harder. I would not tell him this as it would not change his judgment and would only make me seem inferior in his eyes. What he knows he knows, and there is little changing that. It is actually one of his best qualities. Like a rock, he is there immovable.


Other than these entries, there is little else other than notes on neighbors that have visited, servants who are hired and fired, changes of the season. Her frequent letters to her aunt in what must have been the same period seem to have relayed details on the passage of her life. Her communications with herself seems to have been less important until the time she met Gilles de Thorigny. She does not even mention her trip to Paris, although she does mention altering some of the clothes purchased there. Nor does she mention the fall from her horse that resulted in her miscarriage.

She never mentions Gilles de Thorigny by name in her diaries, but at one point there are musings on details of a "friend's" house that clearly indicate (at least to me) that she was in my home. She writes:

How interesting that in some of the old houses in Terrassée one can still see doorways that must have been medieval in their origins, so low are they. In one friend's home I have seen a staircase that mounts for three floors, the doorways so low that I must lower my head to enter. And any man who is appreciably taller than myself must stoop greatly to pass through. These are obviously doorways thought suitable for much shorter people. I imagine men still wearing pieces of armor passing through, and tiny ladies in dragging velvet, even as small as they are, lowering their heads so that their large headdresses can pass through.

And certainly clergy, monks, boys from the school nearby, all in black, robes to their feet for the older men, tights undoubtedly and doublets for the younger men, shoes with their toes turned up. How fascinating to imagine the many, many people who have passed up and down these ancient staircases and to think of what emotions they must have felt. Are these emotions still steeped deeply in these walls and doorways and railings that passed beneath their hands, steps that felt the pressure of their feet?

This most certainly has to be descriptive of the back staircase in my home, which she slipped up to meet Gilles de Thorigny. Now all those doorways have been sealed with hand-hewn planks, perhaps shortly thereafter, and within the rooms the doorways are now shallow closets. There are other doorways that have become closets and cupboards in my house, I now realize too. In both my sitting room and my kitchen are low cupboards; no more than five feet high that surely were ancient doorways to the building next door. Or an earlier building next door, since the priest's house next door was clearly built much later than my own.

Entering the houses on either side of mine one can see that their back walls are nothing more than the outer wall of my own earlier building. Side walls and a façade were built and a roof placed upon the dwelling, but were my house to come down, both of these houses would be open to the winds and air on their backsides.

Legend has it that the old cha teau of Terrassée stood on this hummock in the heart of the village and perhaps these walls with their tiny doorways are fragments left of the cha teau after the Danes destroyed it in the twelfth century. The old cha teau that the Comtesse imagines peopled by much-smaller persons with undoubtedly the same gigantic emotions that she was feeling at the time.

My heart jumped when I read:


While waiting for a friend yesterday I noticed that the soft stone surrounding the window casement could be easily marked. I took out my little pearl-cased penknife and cut my initials in it, close to the bottom of one side. I stood back so as not to be seen from the street below as I did not want to be accused of effacing the ancient stones of Terrassée. But on the other hand, I wanted to leave some sign that I too had passed through this historic place, as there were already a good many initials and names in the stone, witnessing that many other who have stood here, waiting for whom? Anticipating what?


Upon reading this I put down the diary and hurried up the front staircase to what I now thought of as "Gilles' Room" and pushed the voile curtains away from the window embrasure. On the left side I could see initials that I had noticed before and wondered if they could be those of the Comtesse. There one can clearly see a large, loopy "C" and a small "d," and the rest has crumbled where it meets the wooden framework of the window. This is the soft Bourré stone, named for the nearby village where much of the stone was quarried for the houses in this region. Easily cut and mounted in place, it becomes whiter in time. The cha teau of Cheverny, built in the sixteenth century, has an eerie Disneyesque quality because of the bright cleanliness of its stone, which has never required cleaning through the hundreds of years since it was built.

———

I stared hard at the initials. Her hand had cut them while waiting for her lover. I turned and looked at the room. Certainly the bed must have stood in that corner. The only place it could really, and there they must have made that frantic and deeply stirring love (at least for the Comtesse) that fulfilled her life and eventually altered it tragically. But did it really? If she hadn't met and loved Gilles de Thorigny she would have led a same flat round of country events nevertheless. Because of him her life was a tragedy. I hope that she understood that a tragedy was better than nothing.

**Chapter 42**
**The Comtesse's Diary:**
**The Dying Soldier**

Toward the end of the diary, which I reached at the end of the afternoon, there was a dated entry. And since there were few dates in her diary, I believe that she dated it for a reason. It reads 20 June 1839, which, I believe, is perhaps something like a month after Gilles de Thorigny disappeared. It is purportedly about something she had read, but I believe it was about something much, much more.

I have just finished reading Talleyrand's memoirs of his days in Spain during the tempestuous times of the Napoleonic invasions and the Spanish uprising against the French invaders. There is one passage that haunts me and that will live within me for the rest of my life.

In Madrid, as the revolutionary forces were entering the city, all the citizens barricaded themselves in their homes. Talleyrand was staying with friends in their large home on the Avenida Castilla, where a pitched battle took place between the retreating French forces and the invading Spanish. As evening fell the French dispersed in the darkness leaving the avenue to the guerilla troops. There were many wounded and one French soldier found his way into the entry of the house where Talleyrand was staying. Throughout the night he lay there, crying out in pain and pleading for water. Those within remained with shuttered windows and doors, fearing to venture out and equally fearing reprisals from the Spanish troops if they were to care for the dying soldier.

The entire night they sat up inside the house listening to the weakening cries and pleas from the stairs leading into the sheltered alcove outside the entry door. And as dawn broke the cries ceased, and they knew that they had witnessed the soldier's death. Talleyrand does not embroider further and does not tell us how he felt. But the fact that he was able to remain a few feet from someone who was dying and in an agony of thirst and make no effort to succor him or care for him says something about Talleyrand that perhaps we would rather not know.

I could not have done this. I could not have remained encased within that house and listened to someone die so as to preserve myself. The memories would have been unbearable. One hopes that they proved to be unbearable for Talleyrand. I would have had to go outside, even if my host had felt they must close the door upon me and refuse me re-entry. I would have preferred to die beside that soldier. Who knows who may have loved him back in France? And how they would have suffered if they had known how he died?

And are there not many similar situations in our own lives? Where we lay sprawled upon a staircase leading to a world of safety and happiness, and our wounds go untended? Our thirst goes unslaked. And those who could do something about it know that we are there suffering, yet for their own reasons they do nothing about it. Do they suffer equally knowing they are doing nothing to soothe the pain of a fellow human being? Or do they grow used to the sufferer at their doorstep? The sufferer who does not even have the escape of an early death, but who remains there, the hopelessness and the hurt tearing away at them as the days file slowly past.


Can this be anything but the Comtesse commenting on her situation? And who is the person who does nothing to relieve her pain? Was there anyone?

———

# Chapter 43
## The Comtesse's Diary:
## The Mechanical Doll

I searched the diary for some reference to what might have happened the night that Gilles de Thorigny failed to keep his rendezvous with Catherine, but she never mentions it. There is no reference to Gilles except that he must be the friend she refers to so glancingly in her notes on the old building of Terrassée. Her initials confirming that she had been in that room with its view of the abbey chapel of our Lady of the Snows and the thick, shortish Charles the Seventh tower. But she never refers to what must have been the great love of her life.

One of the very last entries told me something of how the Comtesse was able finally to accommodate her life experience and to continue on through a life that was rather a long one for the period in which she lived.

Are we not all then a kind of doll in this world that unfolds about us, season upon season, leaves growing, flourishing, and falling, only to return again? Are we not, too, part of this relentlessly ongoing parade that is constantly changing and yet not changing at all?

Like some automaton, like some mechanical doll, we emerge from our mother's womb. In our youth we worry and fret as to what will become of us, when, in fact, there is nothing to worry about. The person we are will inevitably result in the life that we have. Can we consider character to be destiny? I think so. Did I think of that or did I hear it somewhere? No matter.

Our emotions force us forward, like a kind of Trojan horse, bearing within ourselves our mind which would like to think it is guiding us, but, in fact, is being dragged along willy-nilly where the inexorable passage of the mechanical doll takes us.

Because we must love, we are carried over the roughest terrain doing terrible injury to that soft, unprotected mind within. The mind tries very hard to guide the doll, to counsel the doll, but to little avail. The doll must live out the life that it has come here to live, happy or sad as it may be. And the mind then can do one of two things. It can revise the memories; replace them with events that never happened. It can then have a fictitious history which it recounts to others, and when called to accounts will deny that other less acceptable events ever occurred. This is what most people do.

Or it can remain clear and aloof, a captive in the head of the mechanical doll. Like a ship captain who has lost control of his ship, or the engineer a train, racing through the night with sparks and smoke flying, bound to iron tracks from which there is no deviation. And the doomed passenger, or brain, has no recourse except to observe and accept a passage of life that may be totally unlike what one has hoped for or anticipated. Sometimes from the high windows of the doll's eyes we see a distant countryside, shining under the high summer sun, but that is not where the doll is inclined to go.

And beneath it all, is the doll making choices? Is the doll deciding that its passage through a dramatic and stormy countryside is essential to its earthly passage, and even though there is nothing but an endless desert once the storm is traversed, is it perhaps necessary for the doll to complete its pre-patterned trajectory? And was the sunlit landscape only a mirage, never really there, never a true possibility? Trapped as we are in the mechanical doll that is ourselves, can we accept that the life we have had is the life we should have had? That any attempts to guide the mechanical doll are futile; we cannot direct, we can only observe.

## Chapter 44
## Minette's Entry

From D. D. Abercrombie's Journal:

In the very back of the diary were several pages on which someone had written in pencil. The formation of the letters was shaky, and there were misspellings. And no signature. From the contents, I believe it was written by the Countess's maid, Minette, and in her old age. I am sure that her daughter, granddaughter, and great-granddaughter Mme. Trian all read this and held it deeply in their hearts, knowing that their ancestor had done the same. And I understand why Mme. Trian wanted a high price for a viewing of this diary.

I must write down my memory of that night while I still can retain it. As much for myself as others. So that I can read it and never forget it, as for some others who may in the far, far future read and know these true occurrences.

On that night I set off with the Countess to leave the chateau. I know that she was very unhappy there and that she truly loved Monsieur Gilles, and that I had to do as she wished, whatever happened. I left my own husband and child safely sleeping in our little home and went to the Countess's room at midnight. I do not know where the Count was. It was fortunate that he was not there.

The Countess was dressed and calm and had two satchels packed and ready. We did not carry a lantern, not wanting to call attention to ourselves. I knew that path to St. Marc's across the fields well. It is how all our people from the chateau go to St. Marc. In the darkness we walked, myself following the Countess. When we arrived at St. Marc we went to the home of Monsieur Contant, where there was a light. I had been there before with the Countess. Monsieur and Madame Contant were up and dressed. I rested for a few minutes and departed immediately, as I did not want to leave my own family alone any longer than was necessary.

As I walked up the alley of trees leading to the chateau, it must have been now close to four o'clock in the morning, a figure darted out from the trees and seized me. It was Marie-Therese. My friend from the village who is the maid at the house where Monsieur Gilles resides. "He has killed Monsieur Gilles," she was crying over and over again. I took her to my own kitchen and calmed her as best I could. Sobbing, she told me that she had heard a noise in the night, a choking, gasping sound which seemed to be coming from the room directly below her own. Monsieur Gilles' room. She threw her shawl about her and hurried down the stairs that lead to the door to his room. She hesitated to open the door, but she could hear struggling and gasping in the room. Because she had cleaned that room so many times she knew the door opened directly at the head of the bed, and she turned the knob very quietly and opened the door a small bit. And she saw in the moonlight our Count kneeling over a body on the bed. The moonlight struck Monsieur the Count squarely on the face, she said, and she could see it clearly. She said, "It was like a statue cut from stone. Hard, hard, hard. I ran down the stairs and into the night and here to tell the Countess." And it was true, she was in her nightdress, cap, and slippers with her shawl drawn about her.

I did not wish to tell her that the Countess was gone. For I knew now that the Countess would be back. I dressed Marie-Therese in some of my clothes, and we went to the Countess's room to await her. I explained nothing to Marie-Therese, and she asked nothing.

We sat in chairs without speaking as the darkness grew lighter. I heard a carriage draw up in front of the house and the Countess descended as I went to the carriageway. Her satchels were with her. She nodded and spoke in a low voice to the driver. Although it was not fully daylight I could see that it was Monsieur Contant of St. Marc. I carried both the valises up the stairs behind her. She didn't seem surprised to see Marie-Therese in her bedroom. I didn't know what to say. Finally I said, as she stood in the middle of the room all white, just staring at the window, "I think Monsieur Gilles is dead. Marie-Therese came here from the village in the night. She believes that she saw Monsieur the Count strangle him in his room."

She turned and looked at us. It was terrible. Her eyes were like those of a dead person. They didn't seem to see anything. I was not sure that she had heard me. Then she spoke. "Come," she said. "We will go to the red bedroom. You must bring all my things there." And so each of us brought a valise and followed her down the hall past the grand salon to the guest room, which had very recently been all done up in a new fabric. She directed us to return and bring everything of hers from the master bedroom. All her clothing, her hairbrush, her underclothing, everything.

When the Count came riding in about an hour later she was in bed, not asleep, I believe. We helped undress her and put on her nightgown, even though dawn was now fully at the chateau. Before getting into bed she said to Marie-Therese, "You have been a brave girl. If you wish to stay here with me at the chateau you may." And Marie-Therese did. She was with us all those years until the Countess died. I do not believe that the Count and Countess ever discussed that night. He never mentioned that she was gone from his bedroom. In the kitchen we told everyone that the Countess was pregnant, and that it was very important that she not lose the child. And that was why she was sleeping by herself and had an extra maid so as to not overdo in any way.

Which it turned out was the truth. The Count and Countess were always extremely polite to each other, and after Monsieur Édouard arrived, they made every effort to see that he was correctly educated and comfortable. But it was quite clear that he belonged to the Countess. And that she did not belong to the Count. All I know of this story is what Marie-Therese told me, but it is true that Monsieur Gilles disappeared and was seen no more in Terrassée. But he was not a Terrassée person, and they pay little heed to those who come and go when they are not one of their own.

———

150

# Chapter 45
## The Call from
## the Library


From D. D. Abercrombie's Journal:

Mme. Deneuve called me from the Military Museum library yesterday and turned my world upside down. She was actually quite chatty. "Your interest in General de Thorigny prompted me to work on organizing our historical biographical files," she said. "My predecessor had little interest in such things, and I'm afraid I would have to admit that these files, as well as many others, were not as useful for research as they might be. Many things were simply placed in the files with no real attempt at accuracy and, in many cases, simply placed in the filing cabinets without being filed. I'm sure that she meant to do something about it one day."

I said nothing. What was there to say? Mme. Deneuve did not notice my silence except to say, "Are you there?" I assured her that I was.

"Because of the letters to the general from his cousin that so interested you I kept looking to see if we had any other material. And in addition to those letters that were wrapped in the stocking, I have found something else on his cousin, Gilles de Thorigny. I have found his obituary. There was a file kept on military obituaries year by year, and I decided to correlate them with the biographical files, and there I found both the de Thorignys, the general and his cousin. They both died the same year, you know, 1888."

In French, eight-eight cannot be confused with other years easily as it is "quatre-vingt huit" (four twenties and eight, which sound nothing like thirty-eight, "trente-huit," or even forty-eight, "quarante-huit," but I asked anyway. "Don't you mean 1838?"

"No, no, Madame, you may reassure yourself, it is 1888."

"I will come to Paris tomorrow to look at it," I said.

"I knew you would make something unusual of it," Madame Deneuve said. "That is why I called you." She was obviously very pleased that her news had aroused consternation in me. "But you do not need to come to Paris. I can easily fax you this information. The newspaper is not so old, and I will copy it in my copying machine, and then fax it to you, and if you wish, mail you the copy." Madame Deneuve was all efficiency today.

"I have no fax, but I have neighbors who do and you can fax them," I said, lavishing my thanks upon her.

"I will send you the bill," she said, in closing.

"Oh, please, just tell me and I'll mail you the fifty francs or whatever it costs."

"No, no, I cannot be certain, and it will be no problem to mail you the bill." Madame Deneuve did not want to be spared any of her labors. I gave her the fax number and thanked her again before parting ways.

I called my friends the Terwilligers, who live a short distance in the country, and told them a fax would be coming and asked them to call me as soon as it did. I was badly shaken. If Gilles de Thorigny was not buried in my cave, who was? Had I imagined all this? Had de Thorigny simply betrayed the Comtesse's love and run away? Or did she think he had been killed and mourned him all the rest of her life, never knowing he was as close as Paris all those years?

The phone rang. Mme. Deneuve had been fast. My fax had arrived. I ran from the house and quickly drove to the Terwilligers, a jolly Dutch family of three sisters and a brother, none very young, who live in an assemblage of dogs and cats and horses and sheep and goats in a large brick house. They were not happy that there was not enough room in Holland for all the animals they fancied keeping, so they picked up and moved to France. Most of the menagerie were allowed to stay in the house. They longed to have me stay and chat, but I waved at their round apple cheeks and smiling faces and raced away.

# Chapter 46
## The Obituary of Captain
## Gilles de Thorigny

We regret to announce the death of Captain Gilles de Thorigny on March 31, 1888. The captain was the germane cousin of General Gustave de Thorigny, who preceded him in death by exactly one month, dying on February 28, 1888.

Both of the de Thorignys were graduates of St. Cyr Academy, the national military college. Captain Gilles de Thorigny graduated from St. Cyr in 1833. His cousin the general in 1830.

Captain de Thorigny served intermittently in the army. He was a noted horseman and supervised the teaching of riding at the national cavalry school at Terrassée for a period of time between military duties.

He served with distinction in the brief war between France and Spain in 1839 and was lightly wounded in cavalry action at Perpignan. He later served with equal distinction in the campaigns in Algiers, largely as a staff adjutant to his cousin, General de Thorigny.

A very handsome man, he was frequently referred to as the "beau ideal" in the social circles in which he moved with much ease. His later years were spent in the home of Captain and Madame Etienne Desjardins in Paris. Captain Desjardins had served as his adjutant in the Spanish campaign, and they spent years sharing bachelor quarters until the captain married. Captain de Thorigny is buried in the military burial ground set aside for all graduates of St. Cyr. He lived in a world where his beauty (This is what it actually read, "sa beauté." D. D. Abercrombie) and dashing horsemanship was much noted and appreciated. It is being deprived of much by his passing.

## Chapter 47
## The Comtesse's Last
## Letter to Her Aunt

D. D. Abercrombie note:
This letter was the last of the group given me by the present
Countess. Her son was now about six months old. There may be
other letters extant, but it is unlikely I will ever see them.


14 July 1841
My Dear Aunt,
I am taking Bastille Day to bring you up to date on our lives
here at Le Rivage . The most important news of all is that I have a
son. A beautiful son who is now just a little more than six months
old. He is lying in his bassinet naked in the summer heat, protected
from insects by a gauze hanging from the crest of his little bed. He
looks at his mother from time to time but for the most part is quite
content to examine his own little fists and feet, which are quite
perfect. He is very much a cupid that might have tumbled from a
ceiling painted by Rubens.
He has blond curls and dark brown eyes, the most unusual of
combinations, and his name is Édouard. The Count and I did not
discuss his name as that decision was left up to me. I have always
loved the name Gilles but decided to name him after my uncle, your
husband. He has Gilles among his other names.  He was formally
christened Édouard Charles Gilles Comte Contant de Cazas. Is that
not a nice name and not too heavy, I believe, for my child who not
only proves for all eyes to see that infants come from heaven, but is
also a sturdy and healthy child, already making noises that seem to
be very similar to speech it seems to me? When he looks in my eyes
he seems to wish to speak to me as though he has a message.

My own health is excellent now. When I found myself pregnant in the spring of last year I retired to my bed in a separate bedroom to ensure the safe arrival of my child. I have Minette as the nurse for Édouard, and I also have another serving woman, Marie-Therese, who is my personal maid. She was not well equipped for this service when I first employed her, but Minette has trained her well to dress my hair and care for my clothes. This is not at all the kind of service it once was as I am plainly dressed and rarely visit neighbors or attend social functions now. My duty is to my son. He is my only care, my only interest, my only reason for living.

As you well know, it is unusual the paths that one finds oneself upon as we pass through life. You counseled me wisely in the past, and I do not wish you to think that my relations with the husband that you found for me is one that I regret. I have my child and with his promise, my own life is well worth living.

With all the affection I have always borne for you,


Catherine Countess Contant de Cazas



D. D. Abercrombie note:

This is the only time that the Countess signed a letter to her aunt in this fashion. I interpret it as meaning that she has accepted the title and role that is to be hers for the rest of her life.

# Chapter 48
## The Count


From D. D. Abercrombie's Journal:

Upstairs at the chateau is the large deserted drawing room, which I remembered so well from my visit. The chateau is maintained in a very curious way. Downstairs in the suite of rooms occupied by the nephew and in the recently redecorated dining room all is impeccable. But upstairs in the unused rooms there is no attempt even to clear away debris. In the hall, plaster that has fallen from the decorative moldings is left lying along the floor. No windows are washed. Dust lies heavily on all surfaces.

The drawing room, which is vast, has never had sheets thrown over the upholstered furniture. The small tables still have their bibelot in place, now highly obscured in the all-pervasive dust. The paintings are gloomy and obscure. I wanted to offer a few hours of cleaning to the Countess when she showed me through. Truly, two or three hours with a vacuum cleaner and a dust cloth would have made a huge difference. But I realize that this was not the Countess's house, and perhaps she was showing me the dusty vastness as a comment upon her nephew's management.

On either side of the fireplace were some family paintings and drawings. One I found my eye returning to, of a not unduly handsome man, but whose light eyes in his dark-skinned face made me keep looking at him. "Who is that?" I asked.

"That is the first Count," the Countess said. She leaned over to peer at him as though she had never closely looked at the drawing before.

"Unusual eyes," I said.

"Yes," she said. "They never reappeared in the family again. They say mine are exactly like his, but it is not true. My blue eyes are exactly like my mother's eyes. I have seen pictures of her.

"No," she peered again, "his were quite different. Most of our family have brown eyes, which is curious as brown is recessive. Well, there you have it," she said leading me to the door.

It had been some months since I had seen the drawing room and Count's portrait, but I thought of that space and that face again as I finished the first Countess's diary.

When I ran into my friend, the present Countess, in front of the bakery, I, for some reason, in a completely unpremeditated way when she asked me how my research was going, said, "May I make a copy of the first Count's portrait for my book? I think I'd like to use it as the cover." I stunned myself. I had no idea why I was suddenly asking that question.

The Countess was unfazed. She said, "So you are going to make a book out of the story of our family? I hope I shall have the pleasure of reading it. I'm sure that you know more than I do at this point." She did not seem to be anything more than casually interested. "I'll drop it off tomorrow. I hope you won't keep it too long. It's a family treasure, you know." And she went rushing off, her short white hair almost on end in the spring breeze, her unusual dark-blue gentian-colored eyes twinkling in one last flash in my direction. I had a feeling of real liking for her. It's hard to do with the French since you never really know to whom you're talking.

True to her word, the next morning the door pull clattered the bell and she was on the doorstep, the drawing folded into a newspaper. The Nouvelle République. "Not very nicely wrapped, I'm afraid," she said, smiling.

I thanked her profusely and promised to guard it carefully and return it very promptly. She didn't wish to stay for a cup of tea or coffee as she had to hurry about with all the "commissions" she had to make. I wondered if they were sins of commission. I always wonder that when the French use that word, referring to their errands.

I took the picture to Paris with me, as I was leaving to do some "commissions" myself for a few days. I took it to my framer, a young woman name Dorothée who has an antique shop down the street from my hotel in Paris. I was to be glad that I did.

I asked Dorothée if she could carefully remove the drawing from its frame and have it photographed. She thought a moment and said she believed that the camera shop a few doors down could photograph it and took it into her backroom where she did her framing.

The next day she called me and asked me to stop by. "I have a problem with your picture," she said. "Well, not a problem, but I think there is something you should know about it." I promptly put on my raincoat and went to see what Dorothée was talking about.

No one was in the shop when I got there, and Dorothée came to the door of her backroom. "You are prompt," she said.

"How could I not be when you relay such a mysterious message?" I replied.

On her work table the drawing lay beside its frame and the glass. Also on the table were several sheets of paper, the top one covered tightly with a narrow, neat, upright hand. The same kind of writing style that the old Countess had used, but this was clearly not hers.

"This letter was in the back," Dorothea said. "I did not read it completely through." I believed her. "But it is about a very serious matter. I do not know if you wish to read it or not. Of if you want to keep it, and I will reseal the drawing without it."

"I will take it," I said. "You can reseal the frame after the drawing is copied." Dorothea's face expressed nothing. She was obviously not going to discuss this with me further or ever again. It was not her business, even though she might think about it, and certainly disapprove my appropriating someone else's property. Or was it my property? She did not know, did not want to know, did not want to be involved, and it would certainly confirm for her that people are a devious and unknowable lot and it is best to be as little involved with them as possible. An opinion shared with most of her countrymen and women.

For this I was grateful. And also happy that fate had sent me to Paris to have the drawing copied, and that I hadn't taken it to the photo shop back in St. Marc, where the owner would certainly have read it, returned just as smilingly to me as Dorothée had, then talked about it with every human being in his acquaintance. This, of course, I realized after I had read the letter, which has given me so many new things to now consider.

# Chapter 49
## Letter from a Man
## Who Now Calls
## Himself Count

Dear No One,

This is a letter to no one. From someone who is now even less than no one. From a man who, from this day forward, must play a role. A man who must try to remember how he was before. How he tied his cravat. How he lifted his fork. How he smiled. How he spoke. Before. Before. Before.

I killed a man last night. It was a murder that was almost a comedy. In fact, from many points of view it was a desperate, sad comedy. A comedy in which I will remain forever the poor fool Pierrot. The lovesick fool Pierrot.

I decided to kill Gilles yesterday, before he leaves for Spain. It has become unendurable for me to continue living with a woman who only thinks of another man. The only solution, as I had come to see it, was to remove the other man. As you will see, it was a shortsighted plan. A plan that was to end with Gilles's death. After that, I had no thought of the results, the aftermath. And this is my advice to you, Monsieur No One or Madame, now that I have killed someone, it is important to think clearly about what you will do once the deed is done. For it is then, when your mind is all disordered with the violence that you must have already decided upon what steps that you will take. So that you can follow this plan clearly and blindly because, I assure you, you will be powerless to make decisions then in the state you will be in.

I told Catherine that I had a business meeting in Saint Marc and would be riding back late. She cautioned me about my horse falling in the darkness but I reminded her that it was approaching the full moon and that I would be able see quite clearly, and that in any event the road to St. Marc was dry and flat at this season, and my old horse Rome was good at picking his way carefully. He had no more desire to fall than I did.

I did ride to St. Marc in the dusk. That time between chien and loup, that time when one can not see clearly the difference between a dog and a wolf. That time when one can slip easily from being an old and comfortable dog to becoming a ravening wolf.

I rode immediately back from St. Marc to Terrassée, as it already had turned dark and the moon had yet to appear over the black trees to the east. I stopped in the woods that face the old abbey and tied Rome to a tree, not far from the old stone bridge that crosses the small river that passes through Terrassée. The river that was once larger and wider if one can believe the reports that monks in the earlier times brought in the harvest on flat-bottomed boats on this river, the Sinistre.

I waited patiently beside Rome. Rome was patient too. I had brought his feed bag, and he munched oats quietly beside me. How innocent animals are. They could never plan a murder. It would not be within their power to lie awake in the dark and weep for their sins. They could never sweat and whine about their condition. They are so placid and self-contained. As so few of us human beings are.

As the moon emerged I left the wood and walked along in the deep shadow of the abbey walls. There was no one about, and all the shutters were firmly closed. No lights showed through the chinks around the shutters. Everyone was asleep. In May, the dark comes late so many had probably been asleep long before the light had completely left the sky.

In front of the house I stood for a moment and saw that all the shutters were tightly closed except those in de Thorigny's room. There was no light beyond the open window. Perhaps because of the warmth of the night he had decided to leave the shutters ajar.

It was as though I had murdered before. I knew exactly what to do. Quickly I crossed the street, being careful to step softly and not click the heels of my boots against the stones of the curb or the steps. I pushed the door gently, and it opened. No one had thought to lock it. If they had, how different everything would be.

In the lower hall I removed my boots, and then crept up the old wooden steps, staying close to the wall to avoid any creaking. I removed all my clothes in the little ante room that lies before the bedroom to the left. His room. It was perfectly still. I had removed all my clothes in case there was blood. How did I know to do that? I have no knowledge of ever reading about murder. It was as though someone who was quite habituated to violence and bloodshed was inhabiting my skin. I seemed to know all about doing something I had never done before.

Gilles was lying on his side in the bed with only a sheet over him, his arm and chest exposed. He was not wearing a nightshirt so our two naked bodies must meet in the darkness. There was no avoiding that. I walked noiselessly into the room, the moonlight filtering in, giving enough light that I was able to not knock against some small table or step on some flung down riding boot.

I straddled the body quickly and put my hands on Gilles's throat. Evidently, this is how the person within had decided I was to kill him. I was carrying no weapon. He turned quickly and flung his arm up. I wanted him to see me before he died so he would know his avenger. His long dark hair was flung aside . . . and it was then I saw the man I was strangling was not Gilles. It was a stranger's face looking up at me, his startled eyes already bulging. As he struggled the sheet fell away, and I was sitting astride his naked body. There was no choice. I had to complete what had been begun. He turned beneath me, more in his struggles to escape, and this I can confess to you, Monsieur No One, as no one will ever read this letter, I found myself strong between my legs as though it was a woman beneath me. And as he struggled for his last breath the wetness jetted from me over his round, firm buttocks. How strange we are. How strange we are.

I stood up from the bed. One arm was flung off the side of the bed, and his face was buried in the pillow. He was motionless. I had only glimpsed his face briefly, and I did not want to see it again.

I went back to the anteroom and dressed except for my boots, which were in the entryway down the stairs, and returned to the bedroom. I sat in a narrow chair with arms, a chair that was too small for me, and waited. Now, I do not know for what I waited and why I did not leave then. Perhaps I needed to know why I had killed this stranger instead of Gilles. And in the light that was just filtering in from the very early dawn I found out when Gilles walked in. I heard him throw open the unlocked door downstairs and mount the stairs with no attempt to conceal the banging of his boot heels on the wood. The other sleepers in the house must have been used to Gilles. There was no stirring or calling out. He stopped a moment when he entered the door to the room. He saw me first, then looked at the body on the bed. He seemed to understand in a moment. I saw that he was very much the same size as the man on the bed, smaller than myself.          "You planned to kill me," he said, in a tone of voice I can only call admiring.

"Yes," I said. He didn't move. He was clearly thinking what the next steps were to be. "Who was that?" I inquired almost politely.

"My replacement. I know him. I went to school with him. His first name was Frederic. He arrived tonight although he was supposed to arrive tomorrow, so he was sharing the bed tonight. I was . . ." He didn't finish the sentence. I knew where he had been. With Catherine.

He moved to the bed and threw the sheet back. "No blood," he said. He noticed the wetness on the man's buttocks and drew his fingers across it. He looked at me and said nothing. I moved nothing in my face.

"We must take him to the cave," Gilles said. "And quickly, before anyone else is up. No one knows he's here." He turned the man over and took him by the shoulders, nodding toward his feet in my direction. Gilles was a no-nonsense kind of person. Of course, he was a warrior. He had seen dead men before, and he was used to making quick decisions. I took the man's feet. I hated touching his dead flesh.

We carried the sagging body down the stairs. His head with its long hanging hair flopped between Gilles's thighs as he backed down the stairs ahead of me. He had the greater weight to contend with. One could see quite clearly now in the light coming in the staircase window, although it was still very early, certainly not five o'clock yet.

Gilles placed the body beside the large wooden trapdoor in the lower hall. I lowered my end too, and helped him lift the door and fasten it to the stone wall behind it. "Down we go." Gilles moved quickly down the stone stairs and lifted the body when it was at a level with his shoulders. In the cave he indicated with his head a place against the back wall, and putting the body down, said, "I'll be right back." And ran up the steps. I heard him opening the back door into the courtyard behind the house and in a moment he was back with a shovel. In the corner of the cave beside the staircase he began to dig. He quickly had made a shallow ditch. "Let's put him in here," he said.

"It's not deep enough," I said.

"Here," he said, handing me the shovel. "You dig it deeper." Which I did. We then placed the body in the hole and covered it with the dirt that had been removed. It was a shallow grave, and the dirt heaped high upon it. Neither Gilles nor I wanted to walk upon it to press it down. Gilles looked about. "Hand me the firewood from over there," he said with a businesslike nod.

From the distant corner I rolled the logs, some of them quite large, which he then stacked over where he had buried the body. We brushed ourselves off as well as we could and climbed back up the stairs. We were fortunate that enough light had come down from the trapdoor opening that we had been able to see to do what had to be done.

Closing the trapdoor we turned to each other. Gilles held out his hand. "That was well done," he said. "I am leaving immediately and will take his baggage with me and dispose of it elsewhere. Please say adieu to Catherine for me. I am sorry I cannot say good-bye to her in person." His manner was such that it seemed that I had helped him bury a person whom he had killed, not the reverse. Perhaps he felt responsible since I might have stumbled upon Gilles and his replacement sleeping together, as naked as I was. There would have been some very complicated explaining to do, but no one would have been killed.

I tried to wipe the dirt of the cave from my stocking feet as Gilles went back up the stairs. There was still no sound from the upper floors. I stuffed my feet into my boots and let myself out. There was no one in the streets. Rome neighed when he saw me coming through the wood. He was ready to be untethered. His feedbag had long been empty. He was willing to canter back to the chateau. There was no one up yet at Le Rivage when I arrived, and I put Rome back in his stable myself. I wondered if Catherine had heard me come in. I changed my clothes and went to the kitchen for some breakfast. It had been a long, surprising, and fatiguing night. And there, my dear Monsieur No One, ends my story. Can it be called a confession? With salutations, to you my nonexistent friend, I remain,

Bernard Comte Contant de Cazas

# Chapter 50
## The Return of
## the Portrait



From D. D. Abercrombie's Journal:

When I returned to Terrassée I had the portrait of the first Count neatly reframed and rewrapped among my parcels. I called the Countess and asked when it would be convenient to return it and was asked if I would like to come to tea that afternoon. This was definitely an indication of some new phase in our relationship. The French first meet you in a restaurant, then invite you to a large party for the first visit to their home, then to tea by yourself, and finally to dinner. Very few foreigners get as far as the dinner invitation at home.

The tea was a simple one. The Countess unwrapped the portrait and looked at it as we sipped our tea and nipped on our Petit Beurre, just about the least expensive cookies one could ever find in a grocery.

"One wonders what he was really like," she said.

"I think he got what he wanted," I said.

"What do you mean?" she asked.

"He had a title, a beautiful wife, and an heir. Don't you think that is what most men of that period aspired to?" I said.

"Our title is very shaky, isn't it?" the Countess said as she poured me some more tea. Lipstick had gotten on her teeth, but I couldn't think of any gracious way of calling it to her attention.

"You mean because the first Count married a Countess with a title and took it?" I asked.

She nodded. "I don't think that's any shakier than many others. Titles are just like the officers in a big American company after all, aren't they? They are rewards that are substitutes for money. The kings handed them out to all the people who helped them and kept them on their thrones. The people with titles were just large landowners, don't you think? The Count deserved his, however he got it, in my opinion."

"D. D., you are so refreshing," the Countess said, smiling. "You Americans see things in such a practical way. We French seem to think God handed out the titles."

"God has made some very peculiar decisions in the past. I suppose it's possible. And I think, finally, the old Countess wouldn't have liked being called Madame very well."

"How do you know that?" the Countess asked.

"She mentions in a letter she wouldn't mind being called Madame Contant, but I think it pleased her that her son had a title."

"My great-grandfather?"

"Yes," I said.

"Well, I have always enjoyed having a title, and I probably should just be plain Madame Bavour, but I have always preferred to call myself Countess Bavour de Cazas. That's probably why I divorced poor Monsieur Bavour. He couldn't have a title, and it looked strange."

"What was he like?" I inquired.

"He was a good shot. That's another reason I left him. It began to worry me. He was just somebody who came to the hunting parties. Relatively handsome. Relatively rich. I was eighteen. I longed to leave Le Rivage. And there you have it. I so long to read your book," the Countess said, changing the subject.

"There will be no book," I said. "I'm not writing a book. After I collected all the information I decided there was not enough of a story there."

"That must have been a sudden decision. You copied my great-great-grandfather's portrait only last week for use on the cover," the Countess remarked.

"I know. It just seems foolish somehow . . . My prying into the lives of others," I replied.

"It's the ghost, isn't it? The ghost at the Passage du Salut house," the Countess said.

"I don't know what you mean," I said rather unconvincingly. The conversation was beginning to sound like a Hitchcock film.

"I heard that people fell on the stairs when they visited you. When we girls were attending classes there, someone was always falling on the stairs. Never seriously. But you heard Mademoiselle Cortelage talk about it," she said.

"So did you, but you said nothing," I replied.

"I wasn't going to give her the satisfaction. Her father and she, always trying to take those ugly photographs and snoop into other people's affairs."

"Le Rivage was never photographed, was it?" I said.

"Never. My grandfather hated the idea. And my grandmother was always frightened of that house in the Passage du Salut. That's why she would never go upstairs. For fear of falling as she came down perhaps. All the people who rented it always spoke of footsteps and slamming doors."

"I have never heard or seen anything," I said. "Although my niece claims to have heard footsteps. And people have fallen. Not only on the staircase. That's why I have all the railings and ropes on the stair. I think it's because the stairs turn in a strange way."

The Countess ignored me and went on. "That house always hung there in a peculiar way. I was glad when my brother sold it. We never really understood why we owned it."

"Why did you?" I asked.

"It always belonged to us."

"Not before 1840," I stated.

"How do you know that?" the Countess said sharply.

"The records of the Mairie," I lied. I actually knew of it from Gilles de Thorigny's letters. "It had been an inn before. The Bourdin family owned it."

"The ones who are the masons in Terrassée?"

"Most probably. Those Terrassée families go way back."

"But it has never bothered you, depressed you to live in that house?" she asked.

"Don't you think unhappy lives have been lived in every building?" I replied. "And those lives leave their atmosphere. Their aura. Overall, I think there have been more happy lives than unhappy lives lived in the Passage du Salut house. I don't find it at all morbid."

"Perhaps your good-natured, matter-of-fact American presence has calmed the ghost. You don't believe in it, don't believe it exists?" she said.

"Perhaps," I said. I was eager to go.

"So I will never know why there is a ghost in the house of my family and not here at the chateau, will I?" the Countess asked, fixing me with her birdlike glance. Like an eagle. Certainly not like a dove.

167

"There is no reason for you to know," I said, rising from the table. The Countess followed me to the door and kept her sharp eyes upon me as I got in my car. I'd like to think that for the first time she perhaps thought that Americans are not just overgrown children and are capable of having knowledge and recognition deep within themselves that they will only reveal when they wish to. If ever. Just like the French.

# Chapter 51
## A Last Letter
## from Matt

Author's note:

This letter was fastened to one of the last pages in D. D. Abercrombie's journal with a paperclip. There were no notes or comments about it. But it preceded her last entry.

Dear D. D.,

A curious event in my life which I must recount to you. In my endless quest for self-realization . . . I know, isn't it a bore? . . . I fetched up in Santa Fe last month with a Los Angeles friend who is now living there and we have always shared an interest in what you call "that woo-woo stuff." She has been seeing a hypnotist to recover lost memories and thought I would find it interesting. Which it was.

I think our personalities are very different, D. D. Mine is, I think, more porous and malleable. Perhaps you could say I have not been happy with who I was. You are more like a sheet of glass. Much less permeable, yet fragile. Which is why you tend to leave it as it is and not toy with it. Once broken, never mended.

The hypnotist is an older man who, if not pure American Indian, certainly has much of the blood. He didn't wave a pendulum, but as we sat facing each other I realized as we were talking that I was in some other kind of state than my normal one. I found myself talking about the dream I had in Terrassée where I was telling an older woman that I must go to the war in Spain and she was weeping. The hypnotist interrupted me and said, "And who was the young officer?" And I replied, "Me." And then he said, "And who was the weeping woman." And I said, "My friend D. D." And then we resumed talking about other things in quite a normal way.

———

There are some theories that in our lives we keep
encountering the same personas, sometimes as men and sometimes
as women, until we work out some kind of ancient unhappiness. A
strange idea, isn't it? That we go on, lifetime after lifetime,
interacting with the same small cast of characters. Perhaps we are
not orbiting toward each other, D. D., but away from each other.
And it takes some lifetimes before we are free to seek our own
separate paths.

In some ways I'm sorry that we couldn't have meant more to
each other. But in another way, after my encounter with the
hypnotist, I believe that it could not have been any other way.

In the puzzle that is all our lives, I wanted you to have this
piece. Perhaps it will serve to be useful.

Your friend, Matthew

# Chapter 52
## D. D.'S Good-Bye


Author's note:

This is the last entry in the Abercrombie Journal. It bears no signature:


So there you have it, my friends. Once a mystery is solved there is a flush of pleasure at your own persistence and cleverness, but then comes the question as to why it really matters, this finding of a solution. Nothing has changed. Those who don't wish to know about it will continue to not know about it, so strong is the force of mind.

I think perhaps the old Countess can rest more quietly now. And also the poor man, Frederic, who was in the wrong place at the wrong time and was consigned to a shallow grave in the cave. Their story has been told, however conjecturally. So the Countess's existence wasn't entirely a kind of fraudulent living death. And the replacement riding instructor didn't disappear completely, his existence scarcely recognized, his death unnoticed. I have done that much. And for those who were a party to the fraud and the death, they are not my concern. It is far too late to speak of punishment, and I would not want to be a party to that in any case. Revenge is not one of my weaknesses, even if it is a dish best eaten cold. In this case, very, VERY cold.

I guess the comfort in my own silly life is that I have done something. Even if I am not sure of what I did.

Dorothy D. Abercrombie

## Chapter 53
## Final Thoughts


Author's note:

And so we must observe this kaleidoscopic narration made up of truths and guesses, fact and fictional imaginings. D. D. Abercrombie uncovered highly dramatic events of some century and a half ago, about much of which we will never truly know. It would seem that the Comtesse de Cazas had a love affair with the riding instructor Gilles de Thorigny. It would seem that her only child was his, accepted by her husband as his own child, knowing that he would never have heirs of his own with the Comtesse. And not wishing to set her aside despite her adultery because his own title came, however incorrectly, from his marriage to her.

It appears that his plan to kill Gilles de Thorigny went awry, and an innocent stranger was killed by mistake. And that Gilles de Thorigny, who evidently never had any plan to depart with the Comtesse and was, indeed, on some other romantic interlude the night she fled to meet him, left Terrassée to rejoin his army unit, hence the absence of his horse and luggage. And undoubtedly, he took the murdered man's effects with him. He was to die many years later, having spent most of the last years of his life with the man who had been his young equerry in his army service in Spain.

From the flashes of communication from the past given to D. D. Abercrombie and her young lover Matthew, it would seem one can see hints of the ever-returning encounters of spirits, time after time, through ages past to the present. D. D.'s fascination with the Comtesse, her very presence in Terrassée, may have been some slow, unwinding of some kind of spiritual insistence that mysteries be solved, answers be given. Matthew carried the essence of what had been Gilles de Thorigny, finding as Gilles did perhaps, that his true destiny was with another man. And the ghostly manifestation whom Matt loved in Terrassée, with its dark hair, would have been the manifestation of the man who had been murdered there. A man who may have been a lover of Gilles de Thorigny, a man who may have awakened in the night feeling another man's body on his, only to find that he was not about to make love with Gilles de Thorigny . . . but about to die in his place. And had returned to reach out to Matthew. And Matthew himself may have been some essence of Gilles de Thorigny, returning like some kind of recurring tide to move again into the relationship he had had with the Comtesse, now manifest in D. D. Abercrombie.

One can understand D. D. Abercrombie's decision to move to some city, some country, on the other side of the equator. Perhaps there the movement of past lives would not reach her. Or perhaps there she is seeking a solution so that the searchings, failures, and betrayals will be resolved. So that others in the future will not find themselves relentlessly retracing the paths of D. D. Abercrombie, the Comtesse, and who knows how many others in an attempt to understand the fatal intersections with Matthew and Gilles de Thorigny and their predecessors.

These are only my ideas. Perhaps ideas that never occurred to D. D. Abercrombie, that were dismissed when presented to her by Matthew. I have no idea where you are, D. D. Perhaps someday you will read this, or we will meet, and we can discuss it. Perhaps I will learn more. And perhaps I will understand more about what my own role has been in this. Was I once perhaps Minette, the observer? There is so much to ponder upon here.

# A NOTE FROM THE AUTHOR

If you enjoyed this book, please take a moment to leave a review on the website where you bought it. This would be a great favor to me. Honest reviews let potential readers discover my books. This is a major way in which all writers find new readers. Your review is MUCH more helpful than you might think.

And if you'd like to drop me a line, by all means, please do. I answer each email personally, and love to hear from my readers.

**Email – david@davidleddick.net**

## Several Other Titles by David Leddick

*Click on the cover to go to Amazon.*

*Both Ebook & Print editions are available in all quality stores worldwide.*

# 90 LESSONS TO LEARN FROM A 90-YEAR-OLD

Writer David Leddick has lived multiple lives within his long lifespan. Beginning as an officer in the Navy, he moved on to careers as diverse as a dancer with the Metropolitan Opera, an advertising executive living in Paris, a novelist, a cabaret performer, and several others.

Here are some of the things he's learned along his fascinating journey that you might find interesting and helpful as you make your way through life.

Muriel Hopewell is that new kind of woman: in the Boomer generation, living in a retirement community, still interested in romance. She lives in apartment 2A. She connects with the man living in 2C, who may not be quite who he seems. Between them is apartment 2B, whose occupants seem to die too rapidly, too mysteriously. What's going on? Muriel wants to find out. So will you.

# MY WORST DATE

From the outside, Hugo wouldn't strike anyone as remarkable. In fact, he is much the same as any other sixteen-year-old in South Beach, Miami. He lives with his single mother, hangs out with his best friend, spends time at the beach, is secretly seeing someone his mother definitely wouldn't approve of him seeing, and, while he finishes high school, he is working a part-time job to save money for college.

But Hugo is anything but a typical sixteen-year-old. His part-time job is not at the local pizza place like he told his mother, but rather at a local gay club, where he works as a go-go boy. And the person he is seeing on the sly is a much older man, one Glenn Elliot Paul, whom Hugo met when he walked into his mother's real estate office. And to make it that much worse, Glenn is also dating Hugo's mother.

In the coming year, Hugo will finally learn the truth behind long-held family secrets, brush up against a kind of fame and fortune, and carry on an increasingly difficult affair with his mother's boyfriend. Not wanting to hurt his mother, and equally unwilling to give up Glenn, Hugo is about to experience his best, his worst, and definitely his strangest year.

In the 1950's, seventeen-year old Harry Potter moves to New York's Greenwich Village to pursue a career as a ballet dancer. Professionally, he finds a place as a chorus dancer at the old Metropolitan Opera house and becomes a member of the "Sex Squad" -- those chorus dancers well built enough to carry off the skimpy costumes in *Aida*.

Personally, he quickly becomes the focal point in a tempestuous, complicated love triangle with two of his fellow dancers. Torn between passion and his true love--dancing--Harry must come to a decision about whom he loves, who he is, and what he is willing to sacrifice for the world of ballet.

"Love in the Loire" continues the story of teen-ager Hugo Bianchi, who in David Leddick's novel "My Worst Date" has an affair with his mother's boyfriend.  Now he's doing summer theater in the Loire Valley in France and his mother arrives for a visit with the boyfriend.  There is much distraction with Broadway celebrities and sexy locals mixing it up. Hugo gets a chance to hit the big time and also to find true love.  He learns a lot.  So will you.

Beginning in 1963, David Leddick traveled alone as he didn't want to share his voyages with a fellow American who would make to easier to stay in his U.S.A. shell looking out.

No, he went by himself. He was lonely and alone. But then he felt truly absorbed into the country he visited. Each week he wrote long letters home to his mother with his travels and impressions very fully detailed. After her death he found she had saved all these communications.

He returned to Europe the following year and then during the rest of the decade first went to the South Pacific. He had served there during his duty in the Navy and there were places he had always wanted to visit but hadn't.

---

Now he did. Tahiti, Fiji and more.

Then over the years off to Russia, Sardinia, Mardi Gras in New Orleans, China, Africa and much more, some of them places few Americans had visited at the time.

"It was interesting to see Leddick's take on Paris in the 1960s. That's when air travel to Europe was just getting started." – Leanne Rylander, Liverpool

"When the author went to a lot of these places, Americans were few and far between—a remarkable journey." -Jerry Adams, Atlanta

"He certainly offers a fresh perspective on the exotic places he made it to. Places I can only hope I to visit—someday." – Philip Runmeade, Baltimore

David Leddick made his first international trip from the United States in 1963. He went to London, Paris and the major cities of Italy. In the next two decades he branched out from Europe to cross the vastness of a Russia that had seen almost no outsiders. Then, with a Zen study group, he traveled for a month through a China that was so closed off by its insular Communist regime that the inhabitants had seen no tourists at all. This period of Leddick's travels finished with a deep plunge into the depths of Africa on an extended safari. His fascinating exploration of the Earth, this globe on which he was traveling through space, had begun.

In another decade of travel well into the 21st Century David Leddick explored South America more fully, even establishing a residence In Montevideo, capital of the tiny country Uruguay wedged between Argentina to the south and vast Brazil to the north.

After renovating his 1890s house in the old quarter of Montevideo, he began to explore Brazil, beginning with Rio de Janeiro, following up with a voyage to Sao Paulo.

He interspersed these visits with journeys to Naples in Italy, a favored city. He added to this several sidetrips to nearby glamorous Capri, the Isle where many international travelers go regularly.

Returns to South America led to visits to Curacao, Cancun, and Lima. There were added several sidetrips to Panama, squarely between the north and south continents. He now lives very much midway between the North and South Americas in Miami Beach, Florida.

# A SECOND NOTE FROM THE AUTHOR

If you enjoyed this book, please take a moment to leave a review on the website where you bought it. This would be a great favor to me. Honest reviews let potential readers discover my books. This is a major way in which all writers find new readers. Your review is MUCH more helpful than you might think.

And if you'd like to drop me a line, by all means, please do. I answer each email personally, and love to hear from my readers.

**Email – david@davidleddick.net**